Moving On

A Novel

Moving On

A Novel

Larry Presby

The New
Atlantian Library

ABSOLUTELY AMAZING eBOOKS

Published by Whiz Bang LLC, 926 Truman Avenue, Key West, Florida 33040, USA.

For information contact:
Publisher@AbsolutelyAmazingEbooks.com

ISBN-13: 978-1949504088 (The New Atlantian Library)
ISBN-10: 1949504085

To my family so New England in its roots. My mother grew up on a New Hampshire farm. My wife's family had the famous Massachusetts shoe industry as a part of their lives. All have been endlessly supportive. Our children and grandchildren, now in several parts of the country, have been strong in their love. And to my wife Rosemarie whose love has held us all together.

Moving On

A Novel

Foreword

If you read the first novel *Twice Caught,* you will renew a meeting with many of the same continued characters. In this book *Moving On,* healing from wounds by a jealous neighbor seeking their property, a young couple carries on the past owner's heritage. The high school girl they hire for chores finds herself and her father pulled into threats from a strange local edging for revenge. Guns play a vital part in the lives of this small northern town. Every character is touched by guns – how they can save or destroy.

1

Kurt rested his callused hands on the hoe. He let the sun slide across his face. His shirt was barely damp. This afternoon's chore was easy as farming goes – hoeing the weeds away from the pumpkin patch. In the fall, there'd be plump pumpkins as a sign of the seasons – another one of Lillian's pleasures. Kurt said aloud the farmer's traditional end-of-day relief, "Well now, that's another day. Work hadda be done. And it was." It pleased him that the hoe was one of Harry's farm tools. All those familiar touches gave Kurt a constant connection to the life of the man who had saved him and his brother Logan from disaster in theirs.

Just as they knew it would, the farm had outlasted Harry Kaiser and his wife Lillian – and – Remy LeClair, strange neighbor next door. Truth be told, Ol Remy ended his days in the New Hampshire Department of Corrections as an inmate with a six-year sentence. Kurt and Jocelyn Benoit – Mr. and Mrs. Kurt Slater – had loved that farm for its history, and now it was theirs, a home for the newlyweds. They had read the copy of Lillian's letter to Remy Le Clair many times.

After her beloved Harry's death, she visited her sister in Seattle. There she made her decision about the farm, and it had opened the way for them to own it. They had become that young couple in her wishes. The letter read:

Dear Mr. LeClair,

I should call you Remy. We certainly know each other that well. I am enjoying my stay here. I needed this time. Seattle does not have the winter like we will in New Hampshire. They seem to have rain, not snow, so far anyway.

That's what people do, isn't it? Talk about the weather before they turn to more serious things. I felt it only right to let you know now rather than expecting you to wait until spring. I have had a chance for long talks with my sister Rachel out here and some quiet thinking time. I hope I didn't give you false hope. I have decided not to sell any of our land piece-by-piece. My deepest thoughts and the love for my husband and the history of the farm he cared for so much tell me to delay any forever-decisions. What might be the best outcome is to find a young couple to buy the entire property, home and barn. A couple who would renew its farming use and who would care for it in the tradition. In my dream for the Kaiser Farm, they would have children and begin a new story, one Harry would very much approve.

In the meantime, I may even ask the Slater brothers to move in with me permanently. There is plenty of room. Kurt is an excellent caretaker, and Logan can enjoy Harry's collection in the basement to his heart's content. We will see how that plays out.

I apologize for any discomfort I may be causing you. Perhaps you will come to accept that this is best for you as well. Slicing off some of that land for whatever you might plan then my selling to others -- it probably would not be comfortable for anyone.

Dare I say to you, make good use of your time. I am dedicated to that goal in whatever years God may grant me.

Sincerely, Lillian Kaiser

At first, Kurt and Jocelyn roamed the house as if it were generations of their own family home. They readied the fireplace with birch logs though winter was far off. They placed a framed wedding photo on the mantle. Jocelyn had moved her own furniture into place, but they kept the famous living room rocker, a hand-made Amish treasure Harry had bought on one of his sales routes. Kurt told the story once again about Denise Boudreau, waitress at the Helios Diner. How she had come up to the farm to check on Kurt and his brother Logan. "Why are those boys working up here?" She was to report to her friend, their mother, who had whisked herself off to San Francisco. It pleased him to say that actually that day *Dee was off her rocker.*

They kept the basement collection for other days. Harry's collection remained both astonishing and a woeful crime scene – in that time of Remy Le Claire and his rage.

Moving On

They liked to finish the house tour always with the art studio Harry had added on for grandson James to use that summer. The smell of oils and turpentine stirred Kurt's senses – and his regrets. Kurt had tried to bury those regrets – the pitiful attempted theft of the painting and pushing his brother to be a part of it. He was forever grateful that Harry and Lillian found it possible to forgive. He had convinced himself not to reveal to Jocelyn the regrettable part. For Jocelyn, she would be forever the *Apple Blossoms* girl in grandson James' painting, that full story which had remained secret.

Kurt had let most of his school education slip though his mind like water through a sieve. But from Junior English, one quote by Mark Twain stayed with him, "The two most important events in your life are the day you were born – and the day you learn why." Kurt treasured that life-changing day. He and Jocelyn had finished their regular Friday night date at the Helios Diner, best and only one in that small town. As always, after the meal, they had parked by the river and watched the sunset, west over the Green Mountains of Vermont. As the last gentle rays of the sun eased down, Kurt summoned all his spirit and asked the question. It seemed to him she had been ready with her answer.

Jocelyn was a reader, from Shakespeare to Dickens and back again. Kurt told her she could have been an English prof down at Dartmouth. He knew why she hadn't reached that potential. She had married Bobby right out of high school. They had expected to raise a family. Then that tragic accident – Bobby being killed down at the mill. Did Kurt need any more reasons to love his wife? She did not try to hide those memories. She spoke of them with wistful gentleness. That gentleness and love for her helped Kurt feel that he was carrying forward a great mission – to make the best woman in the world happy and safe.

The girl came out to the back patio, very quiet, not letting the screen door slam. Tracy was careful about all things. Jocelyn had hired her as a house helper, coming some after-school days and on Saturdays. The farm house was huge: Jocelyn tried to maintain the vegetable and flower gardens outside as well, just as Lilian had done with such spirit. Sadly, Lillian had passed on quietly out there in Seattle with her sister Rachel. Her letters had been full of the memories of her years with Harry on the farm.

After Tracy's mother had disappeared – "No doubt off with some loser guy," was the favored story at Gina's Beauty Salon. The potential for juicy details was potato chips in a bowl. Just can't get enough of em. "Probably that Internet again. Meetin' the wrong type. Happens just too easy." And from classmate Lucy Metley, "Oh now, I'll tell you, she was a fast one back in high school." These precious gems from unpolished sources were always said loud enough for all in the shop to hear. Gina and Maureen alertly stored up the best ones to relate as the official version. Bar tenders and hair stylists are always fine sources for lively info and ready counseling.

Mom had been a real mother for a time. She insisted on "Tracy" for her newborn's name. Along with Blondie and Mutt and Jeff, Dick Tracy was her favorite in the comics. Tracy became an only child. There was never a Blondie or a Mutt, though a Jeff would have been fine. Her father's pronouncement came as a certainty: "One kid is plenty."

Moving On

After The Great Disappearance, Tracy lived with her father Rodney. Neither she nor Rodney was very happy about it. But they muddled along. He shopped and cooked. She washed and ironed. Tracy also drifted through her junior year at Coos Regional telling everyone, "I will stay a model prisoner and get out next year. For Good Behavior." Then finally free, she'd promised herself to somehow find her place in the big world. Maybe with so much success, Mom would reappear to share it. For now she was at peace helping Jocelyn and being around adults who seemed at peace as well.

Tracy's task for the day was to clean in the basement – around, on, under and over Harry's amazing Collection. You could set an Antique Collectibles Show in that basement. If you vacuum down there, be church-careful not to dislodge his treasures. Tracy especially loved the First Lady gowns. Lillian had called them her Gracious Facsimiles, recreated expertly by Carol Gerard the local seamstress – Dolly Madison, Mamie Eisenhower and Jacquelyn Kennedy were the choices. Harry had always encouraged his wife to add to The Collection. No manikins for them, but the gowns hung happily and plastic clear-covered on padded hangers. The changes in fashion, the colors chosen were fascinating to Tracy. She was allowed, yes, encouraged, to touch things, carefully of course, and these gowns were special for it. They were welcomed drifts into fantasy. Inaugural Balls – could there ever be a more special night? She would picture Jacquelyn Kennedy and pose, as if she would ever have such beauty and grace. Harry had strategically placed a copy of *Life Magazine* featuring the First Lady next to her gown.

Then on to the animals, Critter Corner she called it. As she dusted, she saw again the preserved toad floating all wrinkly in a bottle. She was definitely not drawn to it. The bear rug surely had a story to tell. So sad that Mr. Kaiser wasn't there to tell it. And someday to give her that comfy bruin rug for her lakeside camp that she would own in her someday-life. Then the milk stool that had been placed with care at milking time next to the cows for all those many years. She knew it would have many stories too, family farm history etched in the wood grains. The farmers had left a sit-indent showing the stool's daily routine. She imagined there would have been barn-cats lurking nearby, waiting eagerly for fresh, warm milk in their saucers.

Tracy eased into the old school desk. On the desk were three books. Picking one up she noted it was covered with brown paper. There were scribbles on the paper and some math figures as if hastily done, maybe being called on by the teacher. The brown paper cover was neatly folded inside the book's hard covers. One fold had a carefully drawn heart surrounding a printed "Harry & Lillian." No "loves", but Harry had cleverly placed the message inside and out of view of the inevitable comments. Somewhere Tracy had heard that kids were instructed to cover their textbooks with paper from brown shopping bags from the grocer. She thought it a neat idea and maybe even a way to recycle, a theme her science teacher dwelled on constantly.

She rounded the inkwell with her finger and thought of the Bronte sisters and their delightful and intense days of writing, perhaps from some kind of Victorian inkwell for a quill pen. She pushed back her brown hair, that piece that just would not behave. Brown hair, brown eyes: with nagging doubts her dad even praised the matched genes from what he now called "the runner-mother." She brushed light dust from her jeans reminding herself how everyday comfortable they were. She resisted dresses and skirts like some people resist snakes and spiders. She thought those choices made her look too short – or maybe too tall. Which was it?

She had heard the required answer enough times in the cafeteria. Especially on pizza day which should have been a treat, she was sure the in-girls were hooting at her. Your head tells you, "It's nothing, probably talking about who is just so handsome or maybe Mr. Dimbo as they called the Algebra1 teacher." But when Britney gave one of her "Ready Girls" signal, the laughter made Tracy certain it was aimed at her. Psychology class had given her what she thought fit so well she had printed it under her photo in her bedroom – Pretty Paranoid. Would people get both parts of the pun?

No stressed boss at a town job to leer over her mistakes, Tracy felt blessed for this incredible chance, a job she would have done for free. She moved on cautiously to the array of guns in Mr. Kaiser's collection. She was instantly uncomfortable. Guns had too many stories to tell. Her father had a terrible one about his dog. His father just up and shot Lucky because he rousted the neighbor's cat too many times. At least she knew this much, she could identify pistols from rifles and shotguns. Mostly from tv, movies and from cousins and uncles. Dad liked all the grand, heroic John Wayne movies.

You couldn't live in rural New Hampshire and not be around firearms. Folks awaited the opening of deer hunting season as if it were a national holiday. For kids skipping school – it was. In the season, sometimes she would open the back door and listen to the booming in the woods. She'd allow herself to worry about a doe and her fawn. Tracy kept those feelings in a secret compartment in her head. Never set yourself up for the classic, "Hey! We got ourselves, sure enough – a Bambi-Lover here!"

Tracy placed her hand on a gray metal pistol, carefully as if it were a sleeping child. She read the tag Harry had attached to it. He had diligently labeled and cared for every item in the collection. The tag read, "German Luger, designed by Georg F. Luger in 1898. Used in WW1 and by Nazi military and SS in WW11." She never would have picked the prized pistol up from its purple velvet placement case. But a strange feeling swept through her. She raised her hand, extended the forefinger and said aloud – "Bang!" Just as little kids have done for years. Who would have been the receiver of that "bang?" No mental picture – no actual person from her life. Surely it could only be classic self-defense. One more hard look at the pistol. What were its stories? She pushed the thoughts away.

"Tracy how are you doing down there?" It was Jocelyn at the top of the stairs. "Enough of this basement. It will always be here. Come up and we will go out in the lovely sunshine."

In the back gardens that lined the patio and stretched to the fields, Tracy drank in the sun as if it were floating lemonade. How did Jocelyn sense that she needed to get away from those guns – and the thoughts that disturbed her so? Of course Jocelyn didn't know it then, but she did seem to have the wondrous gift for always knowing what would be just right for both of them in the daily routine. Tracy knelt down and felt the warm earth on her knees right through the denim. She carefully picked a handful of lilies of the valley. Their white was so dazzling, their aroma so delicate. Jocelyn was busy with the rose bushes. She gently tapped her on the shoulder. "Here, these are for you."

2

Kurt and Jocelyn pulled into the restricted lot. They parked right near the sign: Empty Locked Vehicles Only. The main sign was more ominous – Northern NH Correctional Facility. Even as a kid, Kurt knew of the DOC in nearby Berlin. All kids did. It was just "The Ol State Prison" to them. Kids need material, and the prison gave them some of their best. You couldn't hear the jokes enough times: "You jerk, bet we know where you'll end up!" Reply, "Ya, I'll say hi to your brother." That was the approved response. Especially if you didn't have a brother, it was fine. Do not say, "Be sure to say 'Hi' to your father." Them's fightin' words. And there were some rousing ones. Principal-office levels.

According to procedures, in the screening entrance, the two visitors were frisked by sober-faced guards, one for each gender. His cell phone and her purse were placed in a locker. As per requirements, Jocelyn was dressed modestly in slacks and conservative blouse buttoned to the neck. Kurt in jeans and plain shirt. They had to remove all items from pockets and have shoes and hair examined. Kurt whispered, "Just like at the airport." They waited nervously for the thick metal entrance door to open. "Well, let's see if Remy

LeClair, our ex-neighbor, has learned anything. Can an old dog really learn new tricks? If he follows his nature, the answer is – Not likely!"

The heavy the door closed behind them, like a bank vault, and the guard pointed to a table in an open floor with basketball nets and court lines clearly doubling as a gym. The smell of sweat from years of fierce contests hung in the air. Sitting at other tables were nervous wives and girlfriends, a scattering of restless kids, mothers waiting for sons, the sadness of years on their faces. Jocelyn fought off an impulse to run from this surreal place. Her throat tightened and she could feel her heart thumping. She whispered, "Oh, Kurt – whatever made us think we could do this visit?"

Kurt reached for her hand and said quietly, "Because even his only relative, that wasted Acel, the nephew, swears he'd never visit his uncle. Besides being a jerk, I really think he was in on the trespass crime, if not more. But even a bad guy deserves a visit. It all still bores into my brain. Let's see what the man has to say for himself."

Through the steel door bars, she saw Remy LeClair in the instant-identity prison-issues. Jocelyn held back a gasp. He was led into Visiting by another guard whose face showed military-rigid regulations. The guard pointed to Kurt and Jocelyn at their table. Remy eased himself onto the bench, like the old man he was. After the long time since they had seen him and in this place so alien to them, the sudden, stark intimacy was stiff and forced. More like strangers than neighbors from a time that had turned so ugly. The sight of the prisoner was shocking. His thin strands of hair were slicked back. Kurt realized it was the first time he had seen the man without his hat. More shocking! The bushy-bearded farmer was gone. The lines in his face, never visible before, were deep and unyielding. His chin was soft and weak. They did not know this man.

Before even a simple hello, Kurt just blurted out, "My God, Remy, you shaved off your beard! It was always your sign. Everybody knew Remy, the guy with that shaggy beard." No fun, it was brown so it cancelled any good Santa jokes.

His gnarled hands folded in front of him, always showing as required, Remy stared across the table. He answered in his gruff-voiced harshness, "Guess you ain't been to no prison. No long beards. They think you're gonna hide some drugs or a sharp fork from Cafeteria in there. He smiled wanly and went on, "In the Yard, me an ol Willy told about who we were before these bad years. And he says ta me, he says, 'Now you are Samson of that Bible story. Lost your hair – and your power.' And if I remember his tellin' right, a woman did it. That Willy, he knows the Bible and its stories."

Remy wanted to talk, still looking to take charge even here, "Sure took ya long enough ta visit me. There's lots losers out there -- and a whole bunch in here, for damn certain. Okay, go-head n say it. You Remy LeClair is a big one."

"Well, old man, you brought it – "

"Kurt, please, he's the one now with the pain." Jocelyn was nearly overcome by a powerful urge to reach for Remy's hand – as you would an aging neighbor. She knew she must not. "Absolutely no touching."

Remy managed a half smile, "Didn't bring me no cake

with a file inside? He mimicked sawing away at steel bars. True to form he had to add, "Lousy visit." He looked back nervously at the guard knowing how they always watched. "Got me makin' chairs n stuff in here. Them guard watchers love to shout, 'Hey there, Innie, this keeps ya off the streets.' Reglar hoot that one. They're not sposed to ridicule us." He looked back again and then pushed his complaint, "I probably could write the gov-nor. They outside trump up charges 'gainst inner-cent folk and get big bucks for furniture we gotta make for em?" Remy scoffed and broke into a spasmodic cough. He wiped his mouth on his sleeve. He recovered and plowed on, "Does it say on the cabinet, 'Made by R. LeClair in the New Hampshire DOC?' "

"Well, theses charges against you were sure not made up, were they, old man.?"

"Spose not."

Awkward silence. Then although he already knew the answer, Kurt made direct eye contact and questioned, "Does your nephew Acel visit you?"

Remy's face crunched into a dark scowl. "Not once. Before I was put in – they like to call it 'incarcerated' – I signed my property over to him. House n land n everthin'. Then, smart aleck, he just went off and let the county take it over. Gonna make a park or sumthin'. What'd they pay that sumbitch? I'm in here for six – maybe four if I'm a-behavin'." He raised an eyebrow in a kind of promise. He went on, "I'll never see that park or any money from it either. Truth is – my health ain't that great." He slid his hand across his chest as if to signal where his fate resided.

Kurt said, "After all that you and the Kaisers went through, it seems like maybe a good thing for the land."

Jocelyn nodded her approval.

Remy reached to stroke the beard that was no longer there. "That Acel, more to that story but it'll never be known – by me anyways." Remy clearly wanted to be off that topic. "And what about that brother of yours, that Logan?" He looked at Jocelyn for more approval. "Guess I did lose my control some on that day. Comes to all of us, sooner or later."

Kurt smiled. They had reached deeper levels than he had expected. "He's down at Dartmouth College now. Doing well. Scholarships. Bright kid. That should not surprise you. Things could have been different. You know – the 'what if's' in life."

"Damn wish they hadda been. Every day in this place. Wishin' n waitin' n regretin' – that's what we do in here. Well there's always talk of findin' ways out. Just talk it seems like."

Kurt was on the edge of it – to accuse – to wrench home the truth of dear Harry's so-called accident and heart attack. Just as suddenly, he passed. He would likely get only more angry denial. What was the point? He touched Jocelyn's shoulder, softened and said, "Well, we wanted to come. Seemed like the right thing. Who knows, even Logan may visit you. He likes last chapters." Was that a weak good-bye wave? Or maybe the prisoner was stroking his imaginary beard again.

On the drive back home, Kurt and Jocelyn kept silent for miles. Finally he spoke up, dark intensity in his voice. He repeated what would be both known but forever incomplete, "Crazy Remy charging into Harry's basement – cornering my brother Logan and threatening his life ..."

Moving On

"Yes, Kurt. It torments you. Trespassing and assault, it put Remy in that prison but the truth is – really just too much mistrust all around." Jocelyn softened her voice in that way she had. She said, "I know you believe he likely caused Harry's death."

Kurt answered in a tone near surrender, "That rifle is in some deep lake up north. It all came out in the trial – all but that part. It's too much. I should try to get past it. For today anyway, I didn't feel there was any point to bringing it up with him."

Jocelyn watched her husband, his fixed stare, the tight grip on the steering wheel. She said quietly, "In the end it's all so sad. Is this the best for an old man living out his days? For him, this is now 'home.' I cannot grasp it." Kurt had no answer. He accelerated and spun up some dead leaves on the roadside.

~ ~ ~

Lavalle's Hardware was on Helios Main Street; for business in a small town, Main Street was always the best choice. Andre Lavalle was trying to hold his own against the Home Depot in Berlin, but he knew it could become a losing battle. For now, town locals liked that along with the paint and the brushes, the nuts and the bolts, there were screws of multiple sizes – and – you could buy them in small numbers, not in the usual packaged types with three dozen – when you needed only four. Everyone from wannabe home handymen and moms looking for a gift for Gramps came to Lavalle's. Andre still carried a line of work gloves like the ones Harry used to sell on his New England routes. Andre and Harry Kaiser were great town pals. Harry liked to say, "Hardware stores are a Collector's Dream."

16

The Lavalle's had migrated south three generations back from the tiny town of Trois-Rivieres north over the border, in Quebec Province. Andre's great grandfather Raimond began the business as a General Store and was beloved for his French-Canadian patois expressions which the town fathers found to be quaint, since they were mostly Brit to the core in their heritage. Raimond's required line was, "Me an' family got to here to this petite vil-lage. We hope for not so much neige like in Can-a-da. Eh?" Helios folk pleased themselves with, "Jokes on him. Snow in this tip of New England can blow old Can-a-da away some winters." Their reply in the known routine was, "Now, Raimond, we'll take you up tops Mount Washington some time. Hafta wait till spring thaw though. Sometime in June, if the winter was mild, of course." It was a standing joke, a regular Abbot n' Costello Who's on First routine. It was fun for the store owner and any customer who really came in to get warm. You didn't even have to buy anything.

A hot and humid morning, just as expected in July even in the northern states, Jocelyn brought Tracy with her for her errand at Lavalle's. Tracy loved the black leather in the Chrysler 300 and didn't even push to play the radio. With no local Walmart, Lavalle's was a major destination. Jocelyn had decided it was time to re-do the home studio used all the summer that grandson James spent with Harry and Lillian. He had painted with boundless inspiration every day. He went on to some artist's fame in New York. James' parents were tragically killed in Florida by a DUI driving the wrong way on the interstate.

Now that the house was theirs, Kurt had put up sheet rock on the studio's open wall beams that had held James' framed paintings. He and helper Tracy set in the heavy sheets. He imagined it could be a sewing room for his wife – or even their child's playroom if that blessing came to them. Lilian had decided for better or worse, to take the *Apple Blossoms* painting to her sister's in Seattle. Rachel loved it and Lillian never had told its strange history. The bad or the good. But the charcoal version – done by artist James for Jocelyn as the young girl in the orchard, it hung over the living room sofa at the farm house. Warm and wonderful for Jocelyn – full of mixed memories for Kurt.

Lavalle's was usually busy with browsers and buyers, but somehow Andre managed to give attention to them all. His wife Myra kept the register humming and could tell you every aisle's contents. What did you need – power tools or a fifty-foot extension cord, garden hose or electrical outlets, she had it all at the tip of a request. Kurt had left the paint color choice up to his wife knowing that she would ponder endlessly over the color samples, holding them up to the sheet rock for him to consider too, then tacking up the samples, so she could step back and puzzle even more. "I have to think about it," she said about all decisions. Part of her charm.

Myra made sure Jocelyn knew the aisle for paint. By the time she and Tracy reached it, Andre was already there. He hovered pleasantly while she pulled out her samples and puzzled again over the choices. Finally he nudged her a bit, "Ya can't go wrong with Behr. Think about it, good bear logo and good reputation." Jocelyn finally chose the Behr in Patient White. "That off-white shade will lighten the room up. It'll be soft and take the morning light."

Tracy was always cautious about speaking up, but she

could not resist. "The 'patient' part suits you too."

Andre lifted the cans down, and as part of his style, always found time for a fun joke. They were near the aisle for house fans. He pointed to the row of them and said, "What did the air conditioner say to the man?" He waited for the required nonplussed look, then provided the punch line, "I'm your biggest fan!" Jocelyn and Tracy both smiled enough, so Andre went right along to his next one. "So here's another. Which is faster – heat or cold? Heat! – Because you can catch a cold!" He walked away chuckling and very pleased with himself. Captive audiences and good humor were part of the business.

Jocelyn placed the heavy cans on the counter and Myra began to ring up them up. Even though the store was pleasantly cool with AC, she wiped her brow and offered the expected, "Hot nuff for ya? H'mm let me see, Andre is telling the heat or cold joke today? You can count on one for certain."

Jocelyn nodded and said, "Well everyone knows the jokes are half the reason to come to Lavalle's, and today, a good future customer intro for Tracy, my home helper here. Tracy gave a little half wave and was clearly pleased to be a part of the whole exchange.

Myra took the cash and commented more on the weather, of course, "Need some rain or my lawn will be brown before August." Then she became very serious, "We surely appreciate your business, Mrs. Slater. Uh, Jocelyn. Of course we all know you." Then she checked to see where he was and added quietly, "Don't ever say it around Andre, but we are struggling. Ace Hardware has contacted us, but we are unsure at this point. Home Depot over in Berlin is so big and full of inventory. Not certain if even the Ace brand will hold them off. Got to do something or Lavalle's may be on its last run." She paused to consider the thought once again. She said wistfully, "Grampa would turn over in his grave. Whole town knew him and loved to call him Pops."

Along the sidewalk back to the car, Tracy said, "My father goes to Lavalle's. He always says 'support the locals.' He'd be real sorry to see that store close."

Jocelyn opened the car trunk and placed the cans in carefully. In the driver's seat before she turned the key, she said, "You know, Tracy, you just had a better lesson in economy than you'll ever get from a book. It's very hard for small town businesses to thrive. The big corporations, the franchised ones, are changing the face of America. Who will know you in Home Depot?"

"Or tell customers a fun joke. Or be like everyone's nice friend."

Jocelyn nodded and added, "All those Mom n Pop classics. It's just too ironic. You heard Myra say her Grampa was Pops to everyone."

Tracy enjoyed being treated to adult conversations like this. She offered, "I love that word. Ironic – can't get through English classes without that one. Seems like all the writers can't wait to be sure there is plenty of irony hidden about." She was on a roll and went on, "And what a project just to paint a room!" She wiped her brow in faked strain. "The color choices, the amount you need – and paint costs a lot, doesn't it? When I get my own place, the walls will stay the original paint forever."

Jocelyn laughed, "Not when you see the fading and the scrape marks after awhile. Especially if you have kids hopping around." That prediction caused major eye rolling. Around her father, Tracy had mastered the eye roll. It helped keep the fragile peace. As for kids in her future, she thought becoming an astronaut just as likely.

Now in the summer and school vacation, Tracy came four days a week. This day was a special event – Paint Day. In their old jeans and castoff Kurt-shirts that flopped down below their waists, she and Jocelyn were ready to go. As she popped the first gallon top, Jocelyn said, "I am sure we did the right thing to keep the floor just as it blossomed in James' painting days. All those reds, blues, yellows and tans finding each other. Looks like a Jackson Pollock."

"Hey! I know that from art class at Regional. A class I liked, though I was not good at much we did. Ms. Lowell told us about Jackson Pollock and showed us some of his work. Called Drip Painting, if I got that right. An amazing look came from it."

"Yes, Tracy, but his drips were planned from unusual creativity. James just let paint spot itself on the floor just as it happened. His art was on the easel. Pollock painted horizontally as he looked down on his work. No paint runs with canvasses on easels for him. You are right, the results are dazzling and can make you look over and over."

Tracy ventured, "We make a good team. I know a little bit, and then you know – like all the real stuff."

"Hold that thought. I hear the phone." Back in the studio and clearly pleased, Jocelyn said, "That was Logan, Kurt's brother. He will be coming up from Hanover, from Dartmouth, for a few weeks. He'll keep things lively around here."

"Summer vacation from college? Will be nice to meet

him after hearing some great stories." She straightened herself up properly and said, "That's what they say in movies, those British types, 'My dear, I've heard so much about you.' "

"Tracy, you are a sharp girl, a whole lot smarter than you give yourself credit for. I hope you are putting some of your pay – you know, away for a college fund. And yes, Logan has been out since May, but he stayed on in Hanover to work and take more courses. That one is unstoppable." She added with a knowing look, "Naturally, he did time this return for his friend Kristen being home too."

3

"Listen there, Tracy, I've given you permission to go on this day-trip – with whatsaname? – Logan – Logan Slater. But you better start doing do a whole lot more for me around this home. Up there all the time with those Slaters on that farm. Not all to my liking."

Tracy swept back that one unruly strand of hair, not quite in defiance but on the risky edge of it. She was no grand student, but she had learned to read his signs with uncanny skill: Proceed with Caution – Stop – Entering a Danger Zone. She proceeded with caution, "First off Dad, you know perfectly well I would not be going anywhere with a college guy I hardly know. He invited me to go along, as a treat, a little getaway. But his friend Kristen is going too. She's nice and goes to Middlebury College over in Vermont. You know, maybe it's like part of my rite of passage."

"Rights? Not too many at seventeen."

"No Dad, not right r-i-g-h-t but rite, r-i-t-e. It means a traditional time of moving on, you know – growing up."

So that's it huh? Time with the brainy ones. Maybe some of it will rub off. Ol dad doesn't quite measure up?" He snapped the tv back on. When his lawns were holding, Rodney took his own day off. It had been six years since his wife had done "Her Grand Exit" as he called it. There was finally a divorce and no contesting. Tracy wanted to stay at home with school, friends and all that was familiar. Her mother was happy to leave it that way. Rodney worked hard and they got by, sometimes good, sometimes just okay. Sometimes his day off meant Jack Daniels would come calling. Rodney enjoyed regaling his lawn customers with claims of his local knowledge. His favorite line was "Jack Daniels has got more friends in Helios than I do."

A dozen answers raced through Tracy's mind. She could have given it back at him that she was now earning pay up at the farm – and learning how other people manage their lives. Instead, she strode to the door and – No, definitely don't slam it. She waited on the porch steps for Logan and Kristen. She was now in Safety Zone. No Helmet Required. She missed that Dad had raised his hand in a little goodbye. She knew he was way more bluster than the words.

It was only a few minutes when the truck pulled up to the curb. Kristen hopped out and opened the rear door. She fairly chirped, "Hop up in, Tracy. You are gonna have a special day. Jocelyn did the planning – but we get the fun." Kristen was sharp in her sweatshirt emblazoned with Middlebury and a cap to match in the blue and white college colors. The sports cap sported her blonde ponytail easing out from the back. Tracy's flash thought, "Just like Annika Sorenstam." She got to watch the LPGA when Dad was out, as in really out. Women golfers and with such confidence. They inspired her.

Logan eased the truck away. He swiveled slightly to the rear in the driver's seat to say to Tracy, "How do ya like these wheels! Ram 1500 Crew Cab. Not mine of course. But brother Kurt trusts me."

Kristen punched him lightly in the shoulder. She said to Tracy in the back, "Well, the full story is Kurt told him not a scratch – or he'd be working the farm, instead of the books. Ah, I know he gets it. Logan knows what his brother means. This shiny red baby is almost brand new. A prize possession."

Tracy rested back into the slate gray leather. The rear quad seat was perfect for her. Like a little kid's living room fort. Comfortable and safe. She imagined that a long-legged worker would get dibs on the passenger seat. Riding shotgun – always a big deal. Shorties to the back. She leaned forward and said, "Okay tell me again, we're going to the Franconia Notch to see the Old Man of the Mountain? And then ride a tram car to the top of Cannon Mountain?"

"You will be amazed at the views. My dad used to bring us every summer." Kristen spread her arms as if seeing it all. "All the way to Vermont today if the clouds hold off. We'll walk the rim trail."

"And have cheeseburgers for lunch. Don't forget that!"

"Can you believe it! Logan thinks of cheeseburgers in the middle of the glorious New Hampshire White Mountains."

"Hey, I'm still a growing boy, don't you know. Dartmouth cafeteria?" He touched the horn for a light beep. "It's a challenge some days."

Like his brother, Logan did not talk much as he drove. Full safe concentration. Kristen made sure Tracy in the back was included. She was full of energy in her movements and her conversation. "So Tracy, you know that I go to Middlebury over in Vermont. I'll tell you my story, so you will have some 'up-close-and-personal' impressions. Junior year in high school is when you get serious about college choices. You have done that, right?"

"I did. My guidance counselor, Mrs. Granger, had me in for conferences. Pretty much I think, and her too, the best thing for me is to like, go into the military. I'd choose the Air Force – if I could make that. My grades are so-so, but Jocelyn says I'm like pretty smart from what she's seen. And hard to believe, I'm good at math. That should help." She leaned closer to Kristen. "I need to research way more about the Air Force, but part of the truth is – don't think me weird." She cleared her throat nervously. "I have this thing about guns. Not seeing them but just like the feelings. Dead is dead. That truth. Maybe the Air Force would have less of, like you know, all that direct gun part."

Kristen's ponytail bounced in the cap. "Sounds reasonable. to me. Guns are sure a part of growing up in Helios. A real thing of life there. Me? My dad is all into golf and the only shooting he does is with fancy cameras. Logan could tell you a beaut someday about us going with Mom to buy a classic camera for his birthday. Right Logan?" Another touch to his shoulder.

"That's a promise. Tracy, you will love the details. That's the day I got to drive the Stanton's Buick – how about that – even without a license!"

"I'll hold you to your promise." Tracy answered with growing confidence. Logan treating her like a new friend, she sat back and relished it. Boys had always showed interest, but she usually committed to a careful way out – the old "hard to get." Hard for her really. Never fully comfortable. But Logan was a perfect practice run. So easy to be with – and so safe.

"Man would I like to fly jets!" Kristen picked up the theme and spread her arms again. "The tower would say, 'Captain Stanton, you are cleared for take-off.' " She eased back to serious tone, "Well, back down to earth again, maybe you could do a two-year community college first. Give you time to mature some and bolster your confidence for Air Force testing. I imagine they have some tough standards. Anyway, I think your plan is – well you know, we all have to find our way."

Tracy leaned forward again and almost in a whisper, "There are things at home. You know how it can be. Not so good sometimes. It may take some sorting out for me."

" You and I – we will have that talk someday." She turned enough to catch Tracy's eyes. "I too keep my promises."

"Thank you for that. Between you and Jocelyn, I feel – what's a good word here – reassurance."

"Yes, a good word. Anyway for now, let me brag about Middlebury. Hey – even for just the fall foliage views in the Champlain Valley over there – it's a top choice. Seriously, a very tough school to get into. Great students from all over the world really. And there for a purpose most of em. Not party-out time. She laughed, "Probably it's my sensational softball skill that really got me in. She tapped her fist on the dash to drive the point home. "Coach Walerston – she likes my arm from left field. And I can hit a some, if I can say it." Logan's head bobbed a full you-got-that-right.

Still before noon, Logan slowed on the I-93 where the mountains come right down to the road, the Franconia Notch State Park – winter into spring, a glorious white becoming a green canyon. He made the turn for Parking to

View The Old Man of the Mountain. Kristen was out of the truck first. She opened the rear door extended her hand and said, "Come on, Tracy, stretch your legs and get ready for an amazing sight."

Logan had carefully chosen a parking spot on the line's end to make sure he had only one vehicle next to his to worry about. Always one to be precise, with Kurt's new truck, he avoided being between vans with maybe moms with kids easing them out of sliding doors and too close to his spot. Or some young guy showing his skills by parking tight. No whacks on fenders, please! It was a perfect summer day and cooler in the mountains. Tourists, mostly families and young couples, were lining the viewing spots – and corralling kids who wanted just to run around after long drives. License tags revealed the wide attraction – all the New England states, some from New York and Pennsylvania and even a camper from Nevada and as at all sites, the great travelers from Canada.

"Over here!" Kristen waved the two on to a just-right view. In the lot from the north looking south – there it was. Projecting off the side of Cannon Mountain, above Profile Lake – the gigantic granite face made up of huge boulders into distinctly a man's profile. Tracy pulled her binoculars from the case, focused in and said quietly, "That is so – as you said, amazing. Can't go through fifth grade with Mr. Zelder without hearing about The Old Man. But this is so great actually being here. To see it – uh, him!"

Kristen took her turn with the binoculars. She said, "Even with the detail from binocs, it is still a face, not just a mass of rock. Remember that this formation is all natural – you know, from glaciers millions of years ago."

"Right," added Logan. "Not like the famous Mount Rushmore presidents – they were carved, sculpted." He reached down and scooped up an errant blue frisbee and tossed it back for two boys and their dog to chase.

Another nice tap to his shoulder, "Have you noticed, Tracy, that Logan, he knows stuff. Should be on *Jeopardy* someday. And see what the sign says here, from Daniel Webster, 'Men hang out their signs indicative of their respective trades; shoe makers hang out a gigantic shoe; jewelers a monster watch, and the dentist hangs out a gold tooth; but up in the Mountains of New Hampshire, God Almighty has hung out a sign to show that there He makes men.' "

Tracy wanted to keep up. "I know Daniel Webster from fifth too. Another great man from our state." They read on to learn that the profile had been first discovered in 1805 by a surveying crew. For more recent years in concern for frost and boulder expansion, cement fillers and giant turnbuckles had been installed on the Head to hold it in place. And it was carefully inspected each spring for rough winter erosion.

"From his real estate business, my father knows property, even famous landmarks. Every year we came here, he would say, 'Lord help us, that old boy may crash to the valley below someday. The frost, then the warming and the wind all severe up there.' " Kristen put her hands together in prayer gesture. "That would be a terrible thing for New Hampshire and for all of us who find some sense of peace in that special landmark."

"Yes, it does seem to be defying gravity. But then, no less a figure than Dan'l Webster did say that God Almighty hung it out as a sign. Pretty strong references." Kristen pulled Tracy in closer. "See what I'm telling you. Remember you heard it here first. From New Hampshire's future governor."

Logan did not play into the comment with puffed-up ego. Not his style at all. But there was a sneaky smile and he added quietly, "By the way, back in his time Webster was a top Dartmouth grad."

On their way back to the truck, there were some kids tossing a football around in the parking lot. "See that," said Tracy, "I wonder if it means they are bored – or they're showing their stuff for – you know – their Old Man?"

In minutes they had driven further on 93 to the Cannon Mountain Aerial Tramway and found parking. At both lots Tracy had noticed many hikers with their heavy boots and backpacks. She thought hiking alone, or with a friend, that might be a perfect getaway.

The Tram lot was buzzing with activity on this perfect summer day. More families, more kids. More fathers and mothers, some casual and happy, some bossy and full of supervision, "Stay right with us – or so help me, you're goin' back to the car." Teens and adults were pouring out of a bus – on its side in big letters: Bible Baptist Church – West Hartford, CT.

Just as Tracy dropped to the pavement out of the quad cab, a motorcycle eased right into the spot next to the truck. Logan ushered Tracy and Kristen around to the other side and exclaimed, "Will you look at that glorious Harley! Black with silver trim. Even a dash radio, though you gotta wonder how much you would hear at those open-road speeds."

"Think about that," said Kristen. "Probably for at red lights in town and well, you know, maybe parked under a nice maple for sunset time over the mountains. You and your Harley Honey there." They tried not to gawk, but it was a grand sight up close. The required biker beard on him and muscled arms fully tattooed in swirls centered by a stark skull. The shiny black leather pants for her, flowing dark hair pulled back through a red bandanna.

"Do they ever look the part!" Kristen pushed her hands out to fantasy handlebars and leaned into a treacherous curve. "I got this, no problem!"

"Come on, K, you mean No Problemo. *The Terminator*. Need to love that Arnie Schwarzenegger. And the man could cycle-ride!"

"That series is great," said Tracy. "My Dad and I have them all. He always says too bad his cycle days are behind him now. Well truth is, he never had em, but we do enjoy *Terminator*. She added quietly, "Wish we all had a fearless protector like that."

"This place is busy year round. Tourists for the fall foliage, skiers all winter." Kristen pointed to the left, "Come over here, Tracy. See all those swaths in the trees up the sides of the mountain – ski trails! Looks like some giant had stomped his way up the mountain making his power paths. Even from here, see that some of the trails have kinda like speed bumps. They're called moguls, jumps that give half the fun – if you're real good at it, of course. Like on TV in the Olympic runs called The Mogul event."

First stop was lunch time – Logan's cheeseburgers all around from the Base Station cafeteria. Cokes and chips. They passed for now on the dazzling gift displays, Tram logos on everything from ski caps to napkins. The ticket area walls had stunning photos from the Tram car rides in autumn and the exciting winter skiing. Over fifty trails for all skill levels – Bear Paw for Beginner to Black Diamond for Expert. As they moved to the ticket line, Kristen said, "Mom insisted on giving me the fee for our ride. She was like,' Have a happy day on me.' Just as you put it, Logan, No Problemo."

Tracy thought, What I would give to have such confidence – and a nice mom like that. Her day was full of delight to be with two new and wonderful friends – and in regret – her nagging self-doubts that were always lurking.

They moved forward with the crowd, the full capacity for the cable car ride to The Summit. The guide was easy to spot – young, probably in a college summer job, startlingly red hair in contrast to his carefully pressed green uniform. The three eased themselves to the windows, but Kristen stepped back to let two shorties catch the view. "Seen it many times with my folks and heard the guide's spiel too. But good stuff. Catch it all."

The guide spoke up and the crowd quieted, except the ones whispering about the photo shots they should be sure to take. He launched into a spiel likely given hundreds of times but still with energy as if it were a first: "This car is designed for the eighty of you, but we are tight of course. Try to let kids get to the windows. The ride will take eight minutes. We are an average of twenty feet above the ground as we travel along the cable."

He carried on with the spiel, "The cable is inspected every morning – yes, by a brave mechanic who rides on top of the car. He watches with special care as we ease over the towers along the way. This tram was all new in 1980 when it replaced the older system begun in 1938. First tram ever in North America." He faked a brace against the car side. "Hey, here we go. Hang on! We're going over the first tower." The kids in front of Kristen traded friendly punches, signaling a neat carnival-ride dip. "Yes, on a windy day, between towers you would feel a real tipsy, but naturally we shut down if it is too strong. Always safety first here."

He continued now with good general attention, "As we have reached the midpoint, you will have a great view of Echo Lake to your left, to the north. Profile Lake below the Old Man has disappeared from this angle. You are looking at the Franconia Range of mountains, with Mt. Lafayette its main anchor directly across." Guide tapped his forehead and turned personal for a moment. "My winters are spent down at Boston U., hopefully getting real smart." He chuckled on cue. "If all goes well, I will graduate next year. Then I'm hoping to join the Ski Patrol here at Cannon. Been a skier since I could barely walk. Learned from expert Dad on Mt. Eustis down there in Littleton. The Ski Patrol is an exciting, dangerous and absolutely necessary protection. Snow and wind conditions can change in minutes. Even the best can take very serious falls. Downhill speeds up to eighty miles per hour. Thrills take skills!"

At the summit, most in the crowd followed the signs to Rim Trail Views. Some split off for the inevitable, "Hey, Mom. Another gift shop. We need snacks!" Kristen again took the lead. They let groups and families move along to separate themselves. The rim trail had been kept natural with packed gravel and small tree roots snaking along. There were stubby huckleberry bushes along the upper side all showing endless struggle to survive the winds and harsh winters. Kristen pointed ahead to the downhill side and said, "See how those pines are barely shrubs, the higher you go on mountains, the shorter the trees and then none as it turns to solid rock. It's called the Tree Line." They reached a midpoint along the trail. "Let me play guide again here. We are in effect standing on the head of The Old Man. Well actually, way out forward along that rocky section. They used to have cairns so you could hike out closer to the head, but that choice is long gone. Too dangerous and too much risk to the profile formation."

"Ya, cairns," said Logan. "I know that one. Piles of stones showing the trail direction and way back prehistoric–

Tracy grabbed his arm. "Oh sorry, Logan. But look way across – See! There are hikers walking along the ridge-tops of the mountains!"

"Now hold on there, this Guide was just going to get to that." Kristen pulled them next to a tilted plastic enclosed chart on a pedestal. With her finger she traced the view. "See that biggest one, it is Mt. Lafayette, so dominant from the Tram ride. Then south down the ridge Lincoln, Liberty and Flume. Those hikers are just reaching Mt. Lincoln."

Logan had to jump in. "That's part of the Appalachian Trail. Mr. Kaiser, Harry, my great teacher, has a hiker's backpack in his basement collection. All neat outside pockets for equipment. Got it in a yard sale in Gorham. I still remember that he said the lady who sold it to him told him it had belonged to her father. He'd hiked the full trail. I think about 2,000 miles! From Maine to Georgia. Harry told me that in another life, he would have liked to try it."

Tracy brought out the binoculars. "I can see their packs clearly. They're wearing those brown hiker shorts and one has a walking stick." She let the glasses slide down and did a huge wave. "Ah, they didn't wave back."

"I imagine that their careful footing is the big thing for them right now," said Logan. "But it was nice to bring back some thoughts on Harry Kaiser and his collection. That man definitely changed my life. Another story to hear some time, Tracy. Kristen knows it cause she was there once too." Tracy could tell that Logan was clearly his own man, but there was certainly something more going on with him and Kristen. It pleased her to note these insightful gems.

They walked the trail further and reached the observation platform now on the actual summit. It was structured of heavy beams left as all natural wood. Groups of tourists were pointing at views and assuring each other that "Yes, that must be Canada, way in the blue distance." Kids lined up to put change into green binocular machines that swiveled for chosen angles. Clouds were rolling in at floating balloon speed. They formed giant shadows along the mountain side and into the valley – patches of dark islands that drifted in rhythm with the puff-cotton real ones. "Look now," said Kristen, "you can still just see the Green Mountain range over in Vermont. Too bad – on a fully clear day up here, you can see way into New York and even Canada." Then quietly she added, "Of course these tourists are not really seeing Canada, not with these clouds. Actually we are going to be in a cloud on this Summit very soon."

Back at the Gift Shop, the three wandered the aisles seeking the perfect souvenir. Tracy headed for the racks and racks of colorful logo tee shirts. Logan and Kristen, ever the dedicated students, became heavily involved in the grand array of shelved books offered on every possible topic relating to Cannon and the White Mountains, from ghosts who haunted trail huts, to Olympic skiers who trained on the mountain.

~ ~ ~

One book he opened had a series of photos, some aerial, showed that in times when nature did not supply the expected snow levels for skiing – sure enough, clever man took over. He read from the text: "Giant hoses are dropped into Echo Lake; they pull up gallons of water, up to 3,000 gallons per minute. The water flows through miles of a network of pipes. Aided by pressure pumps, the water finally reaches high up into the ski trails. At mountain elevations, winter night temperatures can be perfect. Sprayed by fan guns, tower guns and land guns, the water at fire-hose pressure is sprayed into the air – and frozen instantly. A team of trail groomers works through the night. By morning, a fresh man-made "snowfall" covering appears, all white and sparkling."

"Like artificial athletic field turf," said Kristen. "Well sort of. Anyway, doesn't this water drain leave Echo Lake way down for the summer swimming season?"

"You asked and here is the answer. The text notes that even in winter, Echo Lake is spring fed and along with huge snow melt-off, it becomes another man-nature balancing act. See – nature comes back to us, no matter what we do to it. Well, that is if we are always faithful stewards. Don't get me started on that thin ice." He closed the book and eased it back to the shelf. He stepped out of the aisle and with concern said, "Uh Kristen, our noses in books, I don't see Tracy. Maybe she found two perfect shirts and is doing a which-one thing. We need to look."

"Some friend-sponsors we are! Find her! She's mature and all that – but these days – just can't be too careful." Kristen moved to the aisle quickly.

Logan checked the tee shirt counter and then up and down the aisles. Kristen came out of the restroom with an agitated stride. "She's not in there either! Very crowded in the shop here. Maybe she wanted just to get some air. I'll head out on the rim trail. You go back up the return route from the summit."

The wind was stronger now and the clouds had drifted into wispy, gray walls. The mountain views had been slowly swallowed up. The rim trail was empty of tourists. Running at fine athlete's pace, Kristen quickly made the turn at midpoint. And there she was – Tracy sitting quietly on the viewing bench. She had her arms folded across her chest against the cooler air. She was staring straight ahead at no scene at all. No expression. Just staring.

Kristen pulled up sharply in front of the bench. Between breaths, she gasped out, "My god – Tracy – what were you thinking!" Anger pulsed up into her throat. She wanted to grasp her under the chin and pour her fear into Tracy's eyes – like once when Mom did it because she made her so scared at a mall. She beat back that urge and stared down on her new friend, "Do you have any idea how much anxiety you have caused Logan and me?" She swept back a strand of hair damp from the run. "Naturally we looked all over the gift shop – including the lady's room! He took the return trail to look for you too, of course." Kristen's anger eased back into big-sister concern. She sat down next to Tracy and said quietly, "Come on now, why didn't you give us a heads-up? Needed air? We would've come out with you."

Tracy turned and found Kristen's eyes. She struggled out, "I am so sorry. You and Logan seemed to be like really into those books. And, well, I'm not a big-crowds person. Thought I'd just walk a bit outside. Next thing I was all the way out to this bench." She twisted her hands together and eased on, "It's always kinda in me, I get to feeling sorry for myself. Thinking about how you seem to have that perfect life – up here many times with your caring parents. Great little sister Vicky to buy presents for and to love. College and a real future to plan out."

She slid away on the bench and dropped her head down. "You know, my parents – Not easy for me to remember after the years. My mother ran off on us when I was nine. Understand – me and my father have got by. Better than that sometimes. But sorry to be sorry, as they say – my father has bad times when he drinks. He can be – you can probably guess it, next day, all nice and saying like, 'We're a team, right?' "

Kristen put up her hand gently and said, "Tracy you don't have to tell me – well, only say what you really think I need to know."

"No this is good. My Dad was a pitcher for the minor league team over in New York, got a contract right out of high school. The Binghamton Mets. Then a really awful – you know – a line drive right off his forehead. Tried to make a comeback but – He talks sometimes about what could have been. Mostly when he's drinking." She paused for the thought, "I have to be real careful what I say then. It doesn't take much to set him off."

Tracy moved in closer and in a voice that held it, she said, "I love my dad and feel so sorry about things in his life – my mother running off and all that – his bad luck in baseball. Most of the time he's real nice. Even over-protective. But most kids think that, right?" Kristen supplied the "for-sure" nod. "We go camping or over to Berlin to shop on a Saturday afternoon. I know he would be in my corner if I need him. Who knows, he may even meet a nice lady friend someday. That could be like maybe a really good turn for him."

Kristen touched her shoulder. Big sister fully emerging. "Tracy, I've seen your inner spirit just from in our short time together. These years will be on by you soon. Even at nineteen, I say to myself – huh! I was all worried about that. Seems pretty minor now." She stood and held her hand out for support. She went on, "Plan on this, you and I and Jocelyn are going to sit some afternoon with lemonade on that back patio of theirs. Lots of ice and maybe crackers and cheese. We will smell the lilies of the valley, we will choose our favorite colors of Lillian's glads. We will talk about life. And we will make some plans that everybody can feel good about – even your father."

4

Rodney bolted up, suddenly awake. A car had screeched around their Emmons Street corner. – can that be some mom whose kid is late for the Little League game – He rubbed his eyes and wondered how long he'd been out. Clock on the shelf showed 2:50. – my god – three hours into the afternoon – He pulled himself up from the recliner. In the bathroom, the cold water splashed on his face was downright shocking. A needed shocking. In the kitchen, a full glass of tomato juice. He wondered again if that hangover cure was mostly an old wives' tale. He downed the juice and put on the coffee. He wandered back into the living room. Next to the clock on the shelf, he was pleased for the umpteenth time to gaze upon his polished high school trophies. He took his favorite one down and stroked its faux bronze surface. Once again he drifted back to those glory days. Coos Regional Hornets – Northern New Hampshire High School Baseball League Champions – 1986. That was his senior year. He went 7-0 that spring season and pitched a 3-hitter in the district championship game. Mostly he whistled fastballs and when needed, a sharp-breaking curve. A left hander, and at 6'2 he could bring it. Coach Ellis left him in for the full game sometimes. Batters from the left side had no chance against that curve.

Moving On

"Strike three lookin'!" Just too easy.

Then the scouts, the phone calls and The Contract. He signed with the New York Mets and was sent to their AA minor league affiliate in Binghamton, N.Y. – the Binghamton Mets. Just right out of high school, he was seen as a serious prospect. Rodney's fastball worked its way up to the low-nineties. He learned a change-up to go with the curve. By mid-season he had garnered six wins, three no-decisions and two losses. Then – in a rocket-propelled-line-drive-instant – it all came crashing down. A ninety-mile an hour fastball pounded dead-on by a batter swinging from his heels. All he remembered was flashing his glove up. Too late.

In the hospital the next day, his buddy third baseman Sandy Nelson told him fans said they heard the whack off his forehead clear up into the stands. "Knees buckled – you dropped like you'd been shot." Sandy had tried to bring a little humor along with his comfort. "Hey, Rod, my man, you ricocheted that baby right to Beasley at First. Best play you made all season." Rodney Rousseau never pitched again, from any mound, anywhere.

Back in Helios with baseball dreams over, Rodney married Lynette, his perfect high-school sweetheart. How could it not be perfect – prom king and queen; star athlete and head cheerleader. After three years of what he felt as dreary grind at the mill, Rodney up and quit. He bought a top-line riding lawnmower and a solid used plow. Had just a little rust. A summer job and a winter one. He'd be back outdoors full time, where he needed to be, and best of all – he'd be his own boss. Maybe he could throw life a big curve.

Then Tracy came along before either parent was all that

ready for a baby. While the daughter was finding her way on to nine years old, mother Lynette had worked off and on as bookkeeper for Mike's Plumbing. In slow times, she got to be downright clever with Mike's Mac desktop. She slid around the internet and found troves of great chat-room chances. The guys even sent photos. Hey-Ray sittin' on his Mustang's hood. Dirk makin' funny faces.

Mom was finding small-town married life just plain "tedious." It became her favorite label for everything she had soured on. There were the ice-box winters that held off spring 'till late April. There was her daughter who had discovered the need for the just right clothes for school – and some testy opinions. Very tedious. And husband Rodney who wanted home-cooked meals, no Hungry Man out of the can. Very, very tedious. Then him plowing storms half the night. Her hating that empty, cold pillow. But in the fridge, be damn sure his LaBatts would be waitin cool n tall at all times. Or else. Or else what? He'd better watch it.

~ ~ ~

And then came the grand bonanza – Big Jamie down there in Texas. He lit up her Mac with the best message and photo ever – "Got a hot Indian down here with your name on it. That's a famous motorcycle, not a feathered Chief. And you're gonna be so hot on it too. We'll be like Willie, On The Road Again! Whattaya say there, wanta be a Biker Babe?"

How could this not be way past tedious! Lynette packed and left, all on a winter's day. Tracy in school. Rodney out on the job plowing the new snow. Stepping off a Delta flight into Texas sunshine. A new zinger of a guy meeting her in the terminal with his certain cowboy hat cocked just right and inviting a, "Let's go babe." Then in the lot outside, his Indian cycle right there leaning carefully on is stand – full sparkling red with silver trim and handlebars and a jump seat for her. Life would surely be good. She fished into her carryon for a scarf for her head. "Hey I'm half way there. Life'a gonna be good!"

Rodney had an inspiration to wake up his day – coffee was just the thing – head's cleared up – should drive on over to the park and watch that little league game – maybe give me some nice memories or yell out some advice – He glided his Ford 150 into the lot right off the first base line. No kid at this level is gonna hit any line drive this far, he assured himself. Owens Field was named for the generous donor who had made his money in the ever-popular skimobiles for The North Country. It was a great field for the teams in the summer, and just right in the winter for the skimobile and snowshoe races. Everett Owens was a good businessman. He sold snowshoes too.

Owens had a stack of wooden bleachers just six high but perfect for eager rooting parents, mostly moms today and a few veteran ballplayers he recognized, like himself no doubt, hanging on to memories. There were always the future really little leaguers straining to be out of parent supervision and back on the ground to run around. Rodney settled in and despite himself studied the pitchers as they came on one-by-one in the next relief turn. He liked that the rules require every kid to get some time on the field and at bat. Even then the right fielder always seemed a bit lonely. Little guys don't hit to right much. This lad amused himself by banging his fist into his glove, as Dad or Coach taught him, no doubt. But the glove thumps were a bit half-hearted. His uniform with National Bankers printed out in bright yellow along the white top told his game story. It was Mom-level clean.

One amply-fed dad on the top bleacher tier just didn't get it. Talk about pressure. Every time his Donnie got his turn at bat, Ample-Dad just had to sound off at multi-decibel level, "Yeah – This pitcher's got nothin. You can do it, Donnie boy!" Opposition or not, the whole crowd held their breath as they rooted secretly for Donnie. If he struck out with the game on the line, his greeting at home could be pretty tense. Fortunately, the coach always took the kids across the street to the ice cream stand after the game, win or lose. Ice cream and your pals can almost erase a bad day.

By the fourth inning, Rodney's back got bleacher stiff, and he eased himself down to field level. Tall guys, they do have their back problems. There were a few fans milling around near the player benches and along the first base line. Mostly fathers or older brothers, some with their glory-days fame on tee shirts: UNH Baseball – Regional Soccer – It Kicks. They needed to be a part of the full scene. They needed to be sure all their buddies heard their brilliant strategy and most definitely every second-guess they could muster. "Man! Knew it! Shoulda left my Tommy in to pitch to that guy." So tempting to let the coach know loudly, "Hey Andy, ya messed up on that one – big time!" At these games one thought tagged Rodney constantly, " geez, just let the kids play."

Between innings, Rodney thought a nice rocky road cone would please his pallet. He ambled up to the gate area. A young guy down the fence line caught his eye. He had on tan chinos and an open camo jacket that looked strangely too warm for the summer day. Camo hat to match. Clunky half-laced boots too. He was on the chubby side but solid. He was facing a woman in a light blue tee and jeans. She was holding up her hands as if to say, "Enough of that. Back off." It just didn't look right to Rodney. Walking up close to the two of them now, he could see that the woman was in definite distress. She inched back. Rodney moved in closer to her and with a thumb pointing back in the guy's direction, he challenged, "Is this guy bothering you?"

"He sure is, I really appreciate your timing. He's a jerk." She took the chance to move behind Rodney.

Easily three inches taller, Rodney wheeled around and came up face to face – angry-player-to-player style. He was leaving no doubt, "Maybe you don't get the obvious. This lady asked you to back off. You need to do it."

Feet at broad stance – arms across his body, face red and already a glistening of sweat, the guy thrust his chin forward and fired back, "Hey! Ain't you that hot-shot pitcher for Regional a few years back? Washed up, huh? My brother played on that team. Don't think he liked you much. Rousseau, right?" Hands now firm on to the hips. Chin out more. "Don't matter anyway. This lady and I was just havin' a nice chat before you shoved yourself in."

"No, no, this was no nice chat." She pointed to the field. "I was waiting for my nephew – tall kid there at third for The Nationals. He's going to have to skip the team treat ice cream. I need to get him home." Becoming bolder now, she said, "This guy just plain invited himself to wander over and – well, he said some pretty crude things." She stared right at him. "He'd better go to some bar for that pickup stuff."

Then came the move. Guy's right hand slipped from the

hip to the belt under the jacket. He whipped the edge of the jacket away – showing the ugly butt of a pistol. Never said another word. Just stood smug and all fake tough.

Smug gone! Tough gone! – Slam! Rodney pinned the guy flat to the chain-link fence. His head at perfect height – Whack! Smacked off the steel top bar.

Back home, missing the end of the game and the rocky road cone, Rodney sat at his kitchen table. He was rattled now that the incident was shockingly over. It all had erupted in a flash instant. He replayed the scene over and over – was he totally stupid – the guy could have – really – what do you carry a gun for – could easily have used it – and then howled self-defense – no – the nice woman would have cleared that up – - but maybe she'd be dead too – these days some pretty strange people out there – glad for one thing – daughter not home –

Then once again the memory that had lingered all these years. Terrible time for a young boy. His father had finally reached fury level that Rodney's beloved black lab, the misnamed Lucky, kept bothering the neighbor's cat. The father took the dog to the barn and with his rifle – point blank, he shot Lucky. Rodney was spared the order to watch it. But it increased a struggled repulsion for that man, his father – and a lifetime hatred for guns. Unlike most all the men in Helios, he didn't own one. And he was sure Tracy never would either. His fathering had its wavering weaknesses, he knew that. But on guns, he left no doubts –

The relief on the phone two nights later was clear, "Mr. Rousseau, this is Carol Girard. I'm sure you won't forget me – or what happened – any day soon. Thank you so much for that – that rescue at the Little League game. You shocked that thug. I found out his name is Willie Martin. I think you put the absolute fear of God into him. He was stunned. Ran off like a scared rabbit."

"Well now, Carol Girard, I appreciate your call." Rodney shifted the phone to his better ear. Maybe you know I went on from Regional to the baseball minor leagues. I had a few brawl beauts in my time there. Pitcher's gotta defend himself after firing one in too close. Batters hate a brush-back. Think they gotta charge the mound and all. Macho stuff you know. So I'm still pretty agile, if I do say so. That smug showing of the gun – I just reacted – big time. I think Willie is out of our lives. He'd better be."

Rodney liked her firm voice, the confidence that came through. She went on, "Truth is I've had some – some unfortunate, well, dangerous things in my life. Now this one – guns and a loser guy together. Not a good combination." As Carol eased to the end of the phone call, she said, "I remember you now, Rodney Rousseau, from school and sports. I was two years ahead." A brief hesitation, then the real thing, "You seem like a nice guy. Well you certainly were at that tense moment. The thing is – I'm not – as they say, not really attached now. If you aren't, maybe you'd like to call me. And just to note it, for the record, I'm a baseball fan too. I know what a brush-back is."

Rodney hung up the phone, settled back in the kitchen chair and let some sunny thoughts stir themselves – this could be a new direction for me – out of the deep rut been in since wife did her grand exit – her big mistake for leaving like that – and mine for letting it get to me for so long – ah now, Carol – happy times there maybe – making that phone call would be good for me – and let's see what happens –

ex-wife – you traded me off for a biker guy – just maybe we'll complete that trade – finding that player to be named later–

~ ~ ~

Back in his apartment, Willie Martin sat with his beer at his kitchen table and struggled on from wildly insulted and furious to careful considerations of certain revenge. How could he be made to feel so small and put down by this guy Rodney Rousseau – and in front of a woman yet. A woman he thought would – well at least be open to his – to his whatever. And why didn't he use that pistol! He knew why – way too open and with people around and all that. There'd be times to come, he promised himself. His head still ached from being whacked into the fence, but it was his pride that really hurt. Just like back in high school when he had mustered the courage to ask Charlene Adams to the prom. Rejected flat out. He thought she even enjoyed the turndown. Great stuff for the girlfriends.

Willie felt that his Glock made up for some mighty cruel bullying he had endured in school. "Silly Willie" was okay for the early grades and the bus. By junior high it got to be shoving him against lockers and some, well, ugly stuff, you know, in the boy's room. He just seemed to be not only target-of-the-day but target-of-the-year. Guys always need one. He fit perfectly. Okay, he was – whatdya have ta call it? – overweight. His mother had soothed him in front of her friends with, "Pleasantly chubby. It runs in my family, you know. His father, the same." Then she'd go on to her God Rest Him which immediately eased the subject right over to his terrible tree cutting accident. Margie and Nona could always be counted on for the "All so sad" rescue. Willie could depart the room on cue.

Now at twenty-three with new height, "chubby became "hefty" and on to what he thought of as "damn-well rugged." He'd love to meet up with old Carl, King of the Bully-Pack again. Would beat the crap outta him for sure. Beatin' would be too good. Maybe plugged – right between the eyes. Clint Eastwood movies were the best.

Willie carried his beer into the living room and eased down into his favorite chair, a humble stuffed recliner in chocolate brown, a few minor stains along the arms. When he tilted it back, he knew a nap would beckon him. The only other chair was a straight-back bargain from Good Will. Well, just in case he had a visitor – yes, like that lady back at the park. Stranger things have happened he assured himself.

He put his empty on the lamp table and began to drift into escape from the day's defeat. As he slipped off, he thought about Mrs. Caniston who owned the building. The day he interviewed to rent from her. ... "Well now really, it's not so hard to remember – Can-is-ton, like canister, those nice tin jars for tea... walk with me through the apartment and know that I have video of every inch. ... sign the lease and be responsible to have it look just like this at the end of your year ...if you're smart you'll watch your drinking and hear this... no loud noise ... no loose women ... small town ... I know them all."

Willie thought the place was just right for him. "Mrs. C.," as she said he could call her, was down the hall in a double apartment she had renovated. Mrs. C. even told him that her husband, may he rest in peace, had left the building to her. After he smoked and drank himself into eternity, she had added, a remark that seemed well used. She was still an attractive woman, early sixties he guessed. Nice gray lines in styled short hair and blouse and slacks usually. Every now and then she had invited Willie in late afternoon for a visit. "Tea time," she always said, "for us Brits."

She always went on – and on – to tell how her father worked the docks in Plymouth. "No, not the one with that rock, the original in England." Willie sensed that she was clearly single now and intended to stay that way, a widow not looking. She seemed to appreciate his company though clever conversation was far, far from his zone of comfort. He listened to her stories and nodded when needed. She liked talking and a "Yes, Ma'am, I know just what you mean" was his major contribution. Eventually though, he had offered his own tales, slanted for admiration or sympathy of course.

He had noticed that Mrs. C. had the usual photos displayed on her hutch. On his first visit, she ran through the family and a photo of her holding a happy sign that read in big letters: "World's Best Librarian." During the tea and cookies she told of the library she had worked in downstate and how she had loved her position. She assured him that she'd still be there if Herbert hadn't passed on and left her this building handed down from his family. Willie remembered that she held up her right hand and wrist saying sadly that it gave her more and more trouble. She blamed it on stamping borrower cards all day and lifting heavy books or sometimes wishing she could whack a few obnoxious characters upside the head. She lowered her voice for a special revelation, " My doctor says I should see a uh, you know, a specialist for maybe carpal tunnel. I'm not likely to do that."

At times Willie fantasized she was his doting aunt, just like in the old-time stories versions. Someone who'd send down cookies to him though that had not happened. Maybe she'd become that someone he could rely on in his life as a single guy. Safe, never any man-woman stuff.

5

They chose an evening so they could watch the sun slide west gently down over the Green Mountains on its magical route. Jocelyn – Kristen – and Tracy. Two supremely confident women and one not-so confident teen. They sat in the cushioned white wicker chairs on the back patio, the favorite place for Lillian and Harry to end their day. The late-day sun floated elongated shadows as it passed over the farm field trees. The gladiolas sliding around the patio's edge waved their colors in the light breeze and teases of smells. There had been an unspoken promise about Lillian's prized glads. Kurt had followed Harry's teaching with precise care. At the end of last season just as the first frost came, he dug up the corms, the bulbs, and secured them neatly in the rows of egg cartons in the cool cellar. Harry had said, "Let them hibernate the winter along with the bears." Harry's folksy humor – always carrying his quiet wisdom.

Jocelyn took the lead. She laughed and said, "Just like Inspector Poirot would announce, 'You all may be wondering why I have gathered you here.' " Blank looks. "You know, Agatha Christie."

Kristen tried a rescue. "She's gotta be British for certain. I have to admit I don't know Agatha Christie. But I do love the Brits. Right now I'm immersed in Wordsworth for my fall lit course. The Lake Poets."

Tracy eased in, "Well, we will read *Hamlet* in my Senior English. At least I know that Shakespeare is British. She didn't add the duh, but the tone was certainly there. "We read *Julius Caesar* in 10th. Didn't like it much. I didn't get all that Roman heroics – men of course, never very happy were they?" She didn't add or *are they* but she was on a roll for her usual level. "Anyway the real thing, from what I hear that one, that Hamlet, is a lot like me. Stuck between decisions – and – always wondering who he really is."

"Well, get ready, Tracy, because *Hamlet* will be a major part of your Senior English. Give it a chance. Anyway, Ophelia is a neat female part." Kristen did a stage pose. She said, "I read her part in class. You should volunteer for it."

Tracy laughed. "I try to slide down in my seat, so I don't get called on. Invisible me." Then it flashed in her thoughts that her graduated friends had fun telling her about Mr. Preston's class version of Hamlet using once again what he had told them about his college acting days. His Hamlet knocked them out. He totally captured the indecision – pacing up and down the desk rows, wringing his hands and pausing for the lines.

"Well now, a perfect segue. No invisibles here." Jocelyn motioned for them to slide in closer. She said, "Tracy, of course Kristen came to me about both the great day you had in the Franconia Notch at the Old Man and the Cannon Mountain Tram. And also that other part of the day."

Tracy felt the familiar tension in her stomach. She and Jocelyn often had good talks as they worked, especially that one on the painting day. But, how far to go with her personal story? To not be so down and yet be truthful. She did what she knew she should. She turned to face Jocelyn directly. "I know I really messed up that day when I went back on the trail without telling Kristen and Logan. But Kristen got me past that and on to what I was – well, sometimes you know just feeling sorry for myself."

~ ~ ~

A fat bumble bee flitted away, leaving the glads for a call to new aromas. It found Tracy's lemonade and began circling for a landing on the side of her glass. Jocelyn went right to action. She stood and shooed it off. She smiled and said, "The bees are not anywhere near as persistent as the wasps. We like the bees of course. The pollen cycle and all." She sat and went on, "Tracy, we all feel sorry for ourselves at one time or another."

Kristen nodded and eagerly added, "I know you think my life is basically perfect and I suppose, yes, compared to many of us growing up, it has been. But I had way too many "be-perfect" restrictions from my Mom, believe me. Probably every kid thinks that way. Especially – well – what is it with moms and their daughters?

Tracy felt a rare comfort easing in. She said, "You both know it's just me and my dad at home. I sometimes wish that I still had my mother there even, well uh, like to you know, to sometimes restrict me. It gets a little tense at times with just one parent. My dad always says he needs to protect me." She forced a laugh. "See the thing is, I don't have the other parent to play off. Some kids I know at school are real good at that one. Especially the kids who have separated parents where they share time with each. My friend Allison's folks are divorced. She says on visit-day Fridays,

"Well, here we go – 'The Three Ring Circus rises again' I think she plays Ringmaster." But really it's sad and you can usually tell the kids at school who have that – what's a good word – "

Kristen supplied the word quietly. "That anxiety."

"I thank God my sister Vicky and I don't have that to deal with. But there are some really complicated situations out there these days." Kristen tapped her glass and swirled the ice cubes. Was this too much family to say? She said it anyway. "Think of Logan. I am sure it is commonly known around our small town that Kurt was basically both parents in his teen years. And still is really."

Jocelyn smiled her approval. "And look at him and Kurt now. Couple of really great guys, if I do say so."

"Tracy picked up on that. She said, "It's likely that my life may get even more complicated, if that's the right word." Tracy sipped her lemonade being sure not to make that clunky empty-glass sound. "There's good and maybe not so good. For certain my dad's drinking bouts have cut way back – the dreaded scenes that used to come on with them. Much better now for me." She paused as if making an announcement. "He's seeing someone. Small town, you probably know Carol Girard. She works as a seamstress out of her home. Men send their wives in for her to let out their jeans." She's known for being, uh, discreet 'bout it. Her word, not mine." She tapped her head noting "dummy."

Kristen could not resist. "I know that need. My Mom calls it APS – Advancing Paunch Syndrome. Dad resists it like the plague. Big gym guy and reads golf mags while he does the treadmill. Way to go, Carol, saving male egos and all. Anyway tell us more."

Tracy went on, "Carol, she seems nice but the complications – well, you know – what if she moves in with us? He has every reason to find someone. But it's my house too."

With nice refills the Tracy Talk eased itself down to, "It really is your Dad's house, his home, long after you've gone on to your adult life."

To get to that adult life Kristen offered to take Tracy over to the Central Community College south to down in St. Johnsbury, VT before the summer was over. If there was time even to the Air Force Recruiter. For Jocelyn's part, she would invite Tracy's father Rodney to the farm for a talk with her and Kurt about maybe Tracy staying over some nights and weekends when school starts. She had said, "You know Tracy, your dad might appreciate some alone time with his new friend Carol. And you – well up here out of the awkward way. If you catch my drift. You can help me get dear Kurt off ESPN and on to some TV girl stuff. Two against one may work." Lemonade and some sterling advice. A good afternoon all around. – if Tracy would get beyond the complications part. At times it seemed she even found comfort in them. All this big-sister attention was certainly seeping in.

~ ~ ~

Over their second lunch of the week – at where else, the Helios Diner – Carol and Rodney were just receiving their order – his a grilled cheeseburger with fries hot from the kitchen, hers homemade chicken salad on a croissant. Resisting a first bite, Rodney said, "Well now Carol, on a croissant yet. We'll have to find a fancy French restaurant for you." Carol carefully avoided even a look that said, "And

57

you might watch your high fat food choices."

"Ah, you and your macho thing, all locked in. My mother used to call them crescent rolls, same thing. But really, there should be a nice restaurant in the area that at least has some French entrees. Being neighbors of Quebec as we are, I don't think Diner French fries or French toast counts."

Waitress Dee Boudreau bustled by to her tables without giving the couple a second look. "Now that surprises me," said Rodney. "Not even a nod from her. That lady knows everybody in town and most of their business. Did you know, Carol, that she had some direct involvement with the Slater boys at one time. Small world. My Tracy working part time for Jocelyn Slater up at the farm that she and Kurt bought. I told you about that and you know the big story there."

"Oh I certainly remember. Harry Kaiser's funeral and that Remy LeClair going to prison for his part somehow. Never did get that story straight. Small world for certain." She took the lemon off the glass, squeezed it into the drink and took a full swallow and added, "I took in Kurt's suit pants for the funeral. He had lost weight, I would assume stress from – call it great sadness for certain. Everyone knew Harry. I had to take in a full size."

Rodney caught her eyes directly and said, "Carol, you amaze me. Your sign says Girard Tailoring, and the whole town sure knows where to go for top pro work. Yet here you are with me mornings doing the driveway and garden lines with a power trimmer while I mow."

"My mother had me on her old Singer before I was twelve. Lawn trimming? Nothing to it. Many skills with eyes and hands. And it gets you done early so you can take us to lunch. And then we can – Carol stopped mid-sentence. Someone paused by the exit door and gave them a penetrating stare. Then he pointed a finger directly at them. He clearly mouthed, "Not over." And out he went.

"My God! That's that creep Willie Martin! Come on, Rodney, let's pay and leave. I'll tell you a lot more in the truck."

Safe in the truck, Carol was still shaking. "Yes," she said, her voice trembling, "he's gone from jerk that day to downright scary now. He drove past my place last week. I was raking leaves in the yard. He slowed down and did that same stare." She slid in closer to Rodney, "Then I saw him in town, right in front of Lavalle's. He was in his truck when I came out. Sitting there with the window open. Arms crossed and smug as you can be. Just like that day at the Little League game. He watched me all the way to my car."

"Damn sorry you didn't tell me this at one of our mowing work times."

Carol leaned forward, "I'm not one to send out help-me alarms too often. Makes you seem weak."

"Believe it Carol, It's damn lucky for Willie that I wasn't with you I would have – I got him good that day." Rodney whacked his fist top of the dash. Not hard but clearly making the point. "Seems like there will be another time. He won't bother you after that."

"Look at me for a second, Rodney." Her face was tight with anger. "No he won't!" She opened her purse and there in its quiet certainty – was a snub-nosed .38.

Rodney found a pull-off spot. He leaned in and clamped his hand over the purse. It was as a father forbidding his daughter. His "No way!" was as firm as cold ice.

She did not flinch. "Yes," she said, "it is my choice – to defend myself. Andre in Lavalle's knows guns. He told me where to go for one and how to be licensed for a concealed carry. Women alone these days have to think about things."

They sat in silence. Then Rodney said, "For you to be carrying a gun in your purse. I don't know, Carol. Along with protection – there can be tragic mistakes. I mean really tragic."

"Of course I know that. But trust me." She eased back into the seat and went to what seemed like a familiar defense, "Like all dads up here, I was taken as a kid out back for target practice. Soon I could spin a Coke can off a stump with a .22 at 50 yards. Sometimes my dad even paid me for my best shots. He taught safety above all else." She softened her tone, "Mom paid for the A's on the report card." She smiled and added, "With chocolates, never money." Carol closed her purse and reached for Rodney's hand. "I am sure you and I will do the right thing. Another punch-out from you would do well. I like us as a team. But if that thug threatens me when I'm alone –."

Rodney took her hand and pulled her in close. He said quietly, "Yes, I like us as a team too."

6

Kurt, Logan and Jocelyn gathered around the kitchen table to open the package. It was carefully secured with strong backing and brought to the farm that afternoon by UPS. Naturally they knew what the package contained, but to see the painting again – it would be a magical moment. Since she was the center subject as the young girl holding those blossoms to her face, Jocelyn got to slide the last covering sheet aside. She held the painting up and said, "There now *Apple Blossoms* – you are home again. Just as James Kaiser painted it all those years ago."

The brothers sat back in their chairs and looked on in silence. The memories were still set firmly in their minds. Kurt broke the silence, " Ah Jocelyn, remember that winter day when I was up to service your Chrysler. And in the yard you held the bush branch down. Even with just its frozen leaves I –"

"And yes, you put it all together. Just as Lillian's grandson James had painted me in our orchard, and of course I had never seen this original. She took it out to her sister's in Seattle and now Rachel has sent it back to us – to its home."

"And that painting was uh – well, my inspiration for – for us." That was Kurt being far more open than he usually allowed himself to be. He had always struggled with spoken love. Partly New England, partly his father and partly his need to be safe from the past.

Jocelyn came to the rescue, as she always did. She smiled and said, "And let's not forget our first date – at the Diner and famous server Dee Boudreau. You kept your cool perfectly." She caught his eyes directly and said softly, "And – here we are today, a very special one"

With his time before returning to Hanover and his fall semester at Dartmouth, Logan had joined a crew at the new Coos County Park. The big up-coming opening celebration needed plenty of hours of clean up. Back at the farm he and Kurt took the late afternoon to mark a celebration of their own: the life of Harry Kaiser. They wanted the return of the painting to keep its message of forgiveness, the kindness that kept them from dark consequences. They walked the trail down to the bridge where Harry's snowmobile had thrown him to his death. They sat on the edge of the bridge and watched the little brook wind its way along, shallow now with limited summer rain that month. Kurt said, "I will forever think there was more to that accident than we will ever know."

"Let's keep going, on down to the river. A better memory for Harry." Logan tried to avoid images of the actual death.

They continued on to the river and sat under a leafy birch tree. They leaned back against its soft white bark. Its branches extended out to the very edge of the water. Kurt found a small flat stone and skipped it along the river surface, quiet and slow that day. "Wow, can still do that kid's trick."

"A stone all the way to the other side. Birches and stones, we're having a visit from Robert Frost." Logan had picked Frost as his favorite poet back in high school. So fully New Hampshire, he always thought. He shifted his position against the tree. "So much has happened to us since that day when Lilian scattered the ashes right here by the river. Ice edge last winter probably took them along, maybe all the way downstream. That would have been fine with Harry I think"

"Yes, you and I and Kristen and Jocelyn with her that day. So strange how things work out." Kurt tossed another stone. They watched the ripples ease away to the gentle current. He said, "What do you think, brother? Maybe Harry in all of his kindness and wisdom – well, maybe he would even want to forgive Remy LeClair. You know, for all his troubled ideas and forlorn attempts to have things his way."

"That's a perfect word for it. Forlorn, ultimately just sad. I have had that sense of it too. Just too much dark in the world. Him doing his final years in prison like that. He never did actually hurt me. Well, physically anyway."

Kurt stood and said, "We probably should head back. But here is an incentive for it. When Jocelyn and I sat with Remy over at the prison that one time, I told him you might even make a visit too. What do you think? Before you go back to school. Call it a tribute to Harry and Lillian and – their ways."

~ ~ ~

This was the first time Logan had seen Remy LeClair up close since that shocking day. That was the day when furious neighbor went wild and tried to corner him in The

Collection basement. Remy shouting crazy Harry-Kaiser damnations for the crushing of his dreams. Now in his prison issues, his beard shaved down to stubble, Remy looked so very old and tired. No polite handshake. The No Touching rule. Logan had thought of dozens of lines to say, but they all seemed shallow now, in the face of these grim realities. For his young years, the whole prison atmosphere was nearly overwhelming. There was a controlled din of the almost frantic conversations between visitors and inmates at the other tables – sad souls trying to bring back something of their safer lives. He could see the woman at the next table was struggling not to cry. Remy looked and then just shrugged as if to say, 'That's what life is – us in here – them out there.' He and Logan just sat and looked at each other in that strange moment. One inside – the other out.

Remy's voice seemed as old as his face. Finally he broke the moment, and as if all were suddenly normal, he said, "Well kid, your brother said you might come 'n see me. Never believed a word of it. And here you are. Truth is, could never figure out why you wouldn't help a man who was trapped down in an old well. All ya hadda do was get me a ladder."

~ ~ ~

"Mr. LeClair – "

"Ah go on kid, at least call me Remy, after all what we went through."

"All right, Remy. With this time in prison to think it over, I am amazed that you still don't get it. If you hadn't slammed into that huge clock and spun across the floor – and down into that well." He paused to put it in the right words. Do not say "nightmares." He said carefully, "I still have bad dreams about what you might have done to me. You were – I can say it now – on a crazed rampage that day."

Remy clearly did not get it. He stroked his beard-less chin once more and said, "And I spose that clock being busted was the worst of it, so far as you and brother Kurt saw it."

"Actually, Remy we had that clock fixed, and then we set it at the exact time you rammed into it – 3:17. It marked the time your life took the terrible turn that, well, it's what finally put you in here." Logan sat back sensing he'd gotten to some of the truth of it all.

Remy coughed a rasping, harsh struggle from deep in his lungs. He gasped and finally caught his breath. He said in a faltering voice, "Truth is, I won't finish my years in here anyways. Been to the infirmary, then one trip to the hospital. Hear it? Doctors say, yes, it's my lungs." He slid his hand over his jersey, slowly rubbing his chest. "Might be doin me a favor. This ain't no place to spend your last days. That's for certain."

"Remy, my brother Kurt and I have had many talks about those troubling times. We have come to a conclusion. As much as you had your even violent opposition over the land, we think had he lived – well, let it be Harry kind of saying this to you – 'I forgive.' "

Remy dropped his head into his hands for a long moment. He answered quietly, "That means a whole lot to me – in here and all." He cleared his throat and continued. He seemed to be a man ready to confess, "Time for me to tell my part too. Truth is, I did fire a shot at him as he crossed the bridge on that day. Sudden wind whacked my protection spot – and I missed up into the tree heavy with snow. Down in a huge rush, that snow came." With some sorrow easing into his voice, he continued, "Harry yanked his snowmobile. It flew right off the bridge into the deep snow." He drew a deep breath. "Guess you know the rest. Whole town knew it. Heart attack got im."

Logan clutched the side of the table controlling an impulse to jump to his feet and yell. He caught Remy's eyes directly and said, "I knew it! We knew it. Kurt and I – all along." "We – "

Remy put his hand up and said, "Wait there's more. I need to finish it. At that time I admit I was – think you could say – downright happy. Didn't have ta shoot 'im. Nature and maybe, could be, just dumb luck took over." He tightened his fist on the table and went on with rising anger. "Then that Lillian, she went back on her say. Wouldn't sell after all. Her letter – it drove me – well, you chose the right word it seems. Crazy. Crazy just powered me. I needed to hurt somebody for it." He looked over his shoulder at the guard. He shuffled his hands as if allowed he would have reached out to Logan. He said, "And unlucky for you – you was it. At the time it seemed perfect, perfect to bring things up even. Down there in his basement. All those treasures. With no Harry for me to get – you was the keeper that day. So I tried to get you."

"Remy, you should finish the whole story. What ever happened to that rifle you used?"

"Can't do no harm to tell that too. Didn't kill him, did I? That gun is up in the north, in that big ol Lake Francis – all in pieces. Down there with the fishes. I'm a careful man and the Chief was at my door too much. Then I go and lose it all 'gainst you – and end up here."

Logan was about to answer when the guard pointed to their table and gave the Time signal. It troubled him that he could not at least shake the man's hand. After this – this telling of so much truth. He said, "Remy, this honest facing up, I think it will give you a kind of peace, yes, even in here."

As the prisoner rose from the table and turned to go, he said, "Maybe you're right. Maybe we had a good talkin' today – for both Harry and me."

7

As Logan with Kurt's truck, Kristen was an extremely careful driver in Dad's Buick. Not overly cautious to the point of poking in the wrong lane, but confident and alert. Tracy would soon try for her license, so these were lessons she watched intently. Kristen and Tracy were on their way back from one of the great promises – a visit to the United States Air Force Recruiting Station, this one on Loudon Road in Concord. Tracy had been nervous beyond anything she had ever done in her sixteen years. Nervous and yet pleased that once again Kristen was showing her real friendship, an older-sister confidence and a special word she liked – mentoring.

The recruiting experience was enough to make Tracy's head swim – but a good swimming in a pool full of possibilities. Airman First Class Emory Townsend was sharp to the extreme in his AF blues. He welcomed them and didn't flinch at all when he discovered that it was Tracy who was "the interested party." Not Kristen who looked and spoke as if she could enlist tomorrow. AFC Townsend showed a video with the exciting and challenging career choices from Intelligence to Logistics to Mechanics. He noted that there were in fact one hundred and thirty AF careers with varying training requirements. Flight training open to only an elite few. In the swirl of it all, Tracy latched on to one that might be her someday – Rescue Support – training for eight weeks at Lackland AF Base, Texas. That would surely be out of Helios and – Rescue was part of her life's mission. Starting with Tracy Rousseau.

Out for the full day and that great first appointment at the Recruiters, it gave the two time for fun stops. Kristen drove them right to Howard's Restaurant in Colebrook for a late lunch. They both chose "Breakfast Anytime" since it had been hours from their early one. After the great ham and eggs, came the real thing – homemade donuts. Tracy enjoyed everything about the restaurant and learned further that it was part of "Historic Colebrook." The town's Main Street reminded her of Helios. Safe and homey. And shockingly unlike any future for her in the military. It was all very overwhelming. Kristen used the time to ease Tracy down and to bring mature focus. She repeated the recruiter's strongest message – "Bring us the most education you can achieve. There are places for high school grads, but some college will be a major plus. The more, the better. Science and math for certain." Tracy was relieved to hear that part. Her math was strong. She would need to face Physics in her final year with new determination. Well, maybe. Always "the maybes" to resist or to be safe.

Kristen used the trip as a special chance to share some of the unusual experiences she and Logan had had on this road – one beaut with her mother. She headed them up SR 145. They passed the sign that read in simple black letters: Dedrick van Deetman – Antique Cameras. She pulled to a safe stop on the opposite side grass. She said to Tracy, "Great story. Just before we were freshmen at Regional, my

Mom took Logan and me on her unusual shopping errand. My dad's a camera buff, and she was able to find the perfect classic Rollieflex for him. From that charming old Dutchman. Not something my father would have pursued on his own, but he loves the camera – and the love that went into the gift. On the way home, a storm and a sudden dash by a squirrel sent us right off the road." Kristen feigned whipping the steering wheel sharply to a save position. "Well, sorry, no save. We went into the ditch, Mom turned her ankle outside checking the car. And! She let Logan drive us out and along 'till we got ice. He drove just fine and was the hero for the day."

"That is like definitely a great story. I can imagine how proud he was." Tracy turned away slightly to say, "That Logan, he's a pretty special guy isn't he?"

"All of that." Then catching the implication, she added, "Well, we both have full platters right now." She eased the Buick back onto the road and continued north. She said, "Anyway, on to the second tale. This highway has two of my best evers. This next one got me an 'A' for an essay in Freshmen English." She laughed and added, "It actually was one of those classics – 'What I Did Last Summer.' Only my title was Rescue at Beaver Falls."

A few miles farther, they reached the Falls and Kristen pulled into the parking lot. They got out of the car for the view. She said, "You can really see the power and beauty of the falls, even from here. I wanted you to be close to nature at its best. See how it crashes down over the rocks. Over a hundred feet back from us here."

Tracy held her hand up against the sun's glare and said, "Let's go down to those viewing chairs. Then tell me the full story." Tracy learned how Logan, in his unquenchable need to discover and investigate, trapped his foot between rocks high up into the falls. And of course how Kristen came to his rescue. She stood and looked down at Tracy in hero mode, "He never stopped saying it to me, 'Geez Kris, didn't have any idea how strong you are.' "

They reached Helios and Kristen pulled off Main to Owens Field. Not for baseball or soccer but for the ice cream stand across the street. As she eased to the parking, she said, "Come on Tracy, this will be our desert. Ending a great day for us." The ice cream stand was a local favorite with the fun name I-Scream – next to a giant 3-scoop logo of a strawberry cone and the rhyme every kid knew from the old days. Printed in bright chocolate color letters: You Scream. I Scream. We All Scream for Ice Cream.

They sat at one of the tables to enjoy the treat, almost like the sign, only with just two-scoops of strawberry on the giant waffle cones. No surprise, even in the August heat Kristen's cone remained perfectly dripless. Tracy was endlessly impressed how Kristen always kept things so casually under control. For her cone, she had to do fast licks to keep the drips from making little strawberry trails down the sides. She needed several vital napkins for the summer ice cream ritual.

Just as they had finished the last of the treat, from the side of the stand, a man approached their table. No cone or soda in his hand. He had a nose big for his face and strange clunky boots instead of sneakers. He was wearing a camo jacket, way out of place for the summer day. His camo cap matching the jacket was cocked to the side. Not warily, but just as if he were invited, he slid right in on the table's opposite side. In full smirk, he said, "Well now, lookey here. I know you, you're Tracy Rousseau. That's cause I know your old man." He leaned in closer to Tracy and said in a threatening tone, "Back a few weeks ago, me and him – we had, well, let's just call it 'a little misunderstanding.' Right by that ball field fence over there. Messed up me and a lady I was tryin to get with." He just sat. No direct moves, just sitting, smirking and staring right at Tracy.

Kristen was superbly calm. She pulled her phone from her purse and said, in a get-this-fella voice, "I am one second from 911. Want to be seen as threatening?"

Startled, Camo Man eased his head back away and stood. Not menacing, but not at all afraid. He said, "Well, no lady. Guess I don't need that, not today anyways." He took one more long look at Tracy and said, "Now, girlie, you tell dad that more days are comin'. Maybe too for that lady he took."

Speechless at this bizarre scene, they watched while the man drove his black Chevy pickup out to the road. They waited for the big-shot tire squeal. But it never came. They would never know either why this dangerous man wore a jacket on a summer's day. He never revealed why – but the threat seemed very real.

Back home at night, Tracy in her usually comfortable bed could not find sleep. She clutched her pillow. She tried to catch the rhythms of her fan as it eased back and forth, back and forth on top of her bureau. The incredible day spun through her mind. The great parts were slashed away like storm clouds by the bad ones. Would she tell Dad? Not with his temper and what he would surely do. And this creep apparently must know about Carol too. None of this can be good. She finally slipped off to fitful sleep – having no plan at all.

Willie Martin buzzed with mixed thoughts about the incident at the ice cream stand. He sat back on his fake black leather couch and puzzled it through. He liked his rented upstairs apartment over the brick-front shop Pet Stuff because as with most Main Street businesses, they were closed in the evening hours. He could park the Chevy right out front overnight – and no one had even stolen his custom wheel rims. He was pleased with his threats to that Rousseau kid. But caving in to a girl with a cell phone – pretty pathetic. Too many people around, that would be his excuse – again. Well good, he did make his point. He liked that "More days are comin' " line. He repeated it aloud several times. He was a man who needed to fasten on a plan – and the confidence to pull it off.

8

Logan pushed his empty sandwich plate aside and said, "Well, Kurt, you make a near perfect toasted ham 'n cheese, I'll give you that. You might just up and consider quitting your day job at Joe's. Give the Helios Diner some scary competition. You and Jocelyn – opening up as K & J's. You as the very cool short-order cook and she hosting the customers with great charm. Don't mind if I say it again and she's a great looker too. You hit a home run with that lady."

"Ya, brother, I think you've said that line a few dozen times before. But truth is nice. And if we opened a diner wouldn't that be a beaut! It'd be the one skill I'd inherit from old Ralphie, our father. Maybe we'd even entice Dear Ol Dee Boudreau to come on with us as waitress. After all, she did preside over our first date." There was a time when all of this would have been touched by sarcasm. But Kurt, now the husband, had changed his ways.

Up at the farm, the brothers were sitting at the kitchen table, where all fine tales are told. A pleasant and needed summer rain spattered along the back patio and over the gladiolas. The flowers nodded their approval. Logan and Kurt had set the time aside to piece together each version of their visits with Remy in prison – visits by Kurt and Jocelyn, and some weeks later, Logan on his own. Now very serious,

Logan said, "Here's more truth – I think Remy Le Claire may be on his final days. He seemed very weak and not well really. He said as much to me. Sent to the infirmary, then hospital once."

It pleased Kurt to see the precious rain drops make their way down the glass sliders to the patio. He said, "A rainy day is right for our strange history with that man. Your time with him shows Remy finally wanted – maybe even desperately needed – a chance to tell his full story. Certainly not like a dying man of religion with a priest. But it seems like we all would want to say what has been grinding in us for a long time." He sipped his coffee, then slid back his chair. "For him to face up to all those sad details, I actually expected we'd never know."

"But that's the thing," said Logan. "We really did know, didn't we? And we had it right. So strange, Harry's angry neighbor did, in a way, cause his heart attack. Remy admitted it to me. Also, in that way of his, he couldn't get up to Lake Francis fast enough to toss the rifle into it."

Kurt slid his chair back in tight to the table. He folded his hands in a signal of complete satisfaction. He said, "Chief Denton put the fear of God into Remy, and after our tour of the bridge and down to the river, I'm going to fit in one more piece in – as we promised ourselves – in Harry's memory. Harry had that great sense of humor. All those well-timed chuckles. I think he will appreciate this plan from – from his place in eternity."

He finished his chef's creation and said, "You're right, this sandwich is very well toasted, if I do say so myself. Anyway, so here's my plan. Jocelyn and I have been wanting to take a little weekend getaway." He stood and moved to the side of Logan's chair for his finale. He said as if it were a grand announcement, "My brother, now hear this, Jocelyn and I are going to drive on north to that very Lake Francis. We'll try out that new tent, cook on a grill and – this is the Harry's Memory part – do a little fishing. I just might pop a hook right on to parts of an old rusty rifle."

Logan stood up next to his brother. Hand extended, he said, "I like it! Let's shake on it. Here's to one more piece of The Story." He backed away to make the point, "A little reality is in order here, isn't it. That lake is acres in size. It's sure not likely you will pull up any Remy rifle parts with your line." He laughed and added, "Think about it though. That ol boy couldn't have thrown them out very far. No baseball arm on him for sure."

"Nope, no arm at all. Remember how I jacked him up on his feet when he was snooping around in the window." He put his arm around his brother and added quietly, "But who knows, the night air, the quiet wash of the lake to the shore and warm sleeping bags – it might bring us closer to the possibilities of an Uncle Logan to our lives. "

~ ~ ~

In the rear quad seat of the Ram, he and Jocelyn had carefully packed for a cold night – along with enough food for a small army were two Coleman lanterns, extra jackets and sleeping bags. Although the weather reports were for clear days, they included ponchos. They brought insect repellant for the predicable invasion and sun bloc for the wish for it. Of course included was the carefully checked first aid kit. They knew not to be fooled by the warm summer day or the unwanted fish hook cracking through a finger. His boss Joe had a cabin in northern Maine and regaled any customer who would listen about making sure he had plenty of wood for a morning fire up there. Think it's summer? Try 42 degrees.

Some firewood, the tent and the fishing gear were in the cargo bed covered with a tarp. Jocelyn had her copy of *Jane Eyre*, a well-read favorite for years. She made Kurt bring something more than his car magazines. She hoped he would read some of Steven Kroll's *Lewis and Clark*. He always said Mr. Weston in junior year American History was the only teacher who caught his usually wandering attention. That brave exploration of the West. He even remembered Sacagawea, the Indian guide – one of the many strong women in history. Jocelyn enjoyed reminding him of that easily forgotten gem.

Kurt chose the more scenic route north to Lake Francis. They passed open-field dairy cows, heads down and lost in their pursuit to chomp every last blade of the still wet grass. They were Holsteins with the classic black and white markings and common on the remaining area farms. Silver birches leaned out over the road. Acres of New Hampshire pines and firs of all shapes and sizes caught the early breeze.

As the morning warmed, the truck's AC purred quietly. They both wore matching fish print shirts as one more hope for that part of the trip. Kurt had said, if you can't find it in Bass Pro Shops, it doesn't exist. He had driven to Gorham and found the store to be a sportsman's haven. Kurt had vague memories of fishing with his father as a kid and knew he could at least bait and cast. But over the years, he did not even own a fishing pole and gear. The sales guy, Steve, patiently gave him the fisherman's full tour. Kurt had wondered later to Jocelyn if Steve had said after he was gone, "Hey, Mike, can you believe it! A small town guy who didn't know beans even about lures.

But watch him pull up an amateur's prize fish. Always the way. Right, Mikey?"

They found their reserved campsite and pitched the tent on the sensible wood platform provided. No cold or uneven or wet ground and no pesky ants. They were just a few yards back from the stunning view of the lake. From camp chairs, they spent the morning each with pole and lure. After an hour of classic no luck, Kurt suddenly yelled, "Hey, Joce!, Got something real heavy on my line. Maybe it's weird Remy's rifle!"

"Sure it is," laughed Jocelyn. "But reel away." On his line, breaking the quiet water, came up dripping, a sad sight – a caved in and battered storage crate. Kurt pulled it in as one less careless piece of thoughtless discard. By afternoon, they agreed that renting a canoe and easing over the gentle water was a far better choice than no-luck fishing. The sun shimmered across the surface which was clear enough to see into some depths. No fish came to visit the canoe, some weeds drifted under it, and soon they found a rhythm in the paddling. No thrown rifle parts showed themselves.

After hot dogs cooked on a grill over the half barrels provided, they enjoyed two hours of reading time until the darkness eased in. A half moon reflected its glassy silver light across the water. Warm in the tent in the sleeping bags, they rediscovered from kid days what sleeping outdoors in the real night was like. Quiet but for the songs of frogs and crickets in rhythmic competition. Not once did the topic of Tracy and her concerns or Joe at work in his certain fussing that maybe it would be one more year before he would fold. It was a prediction he had carefully protected for the full fifteen years of the business. The best of the trip was that an Uncle Logan may have moved closer from wish to reality.

9

Over the years locals had asked Andre over and over why he didn't carry a line of guns and ammunition in his Lavalle's Hardware. In rural New Hampshire it promised to be a great seller. He had given it serious consideration, but the state and local requirements and regulations discouraged him. Permits, Federal registrations and all. There was also the store's good will to consider too. There was some scattered antigun sentiment in the town, and Dr. Evan Ambrose was especially vocal.

Myra always said she was "dead set against it." Neither Andre nor his wife found the phrase to be oddly ironic. She was fine with the deer season and the needs for hunters and the right to own and even carry for protection. But she passed it off as she was reluctant to have the store be the place for what she called "that gun crowd" though she was unclear who they might be. Her most serious objection was that the wrong person would become a gun owner – and – she could not finish with any detail. The images from the news and the endless versions on TV filled them in. She knew that there was violence "out there," but having an incident in their hometown and worse, a direct connection to the store – it unnerved Myra. She knew these fears were what fears often can be: irrational. But they do linger.

Moving On

Keeping the family tradition, Lavalle's was closed on Sundays. Anyone with hardware needs knew that they must be in by Saturday. After the nine o'clock service at St. John's, Andre bought the Sunday *Manchester Union* at the Mobil station, and at home Myra cooked a special breakfast. What was today's hankering? Choose it – scrambled, fried over medium, omelet, omelet with cheese and the works, and of course lots of crispy bacon. Toast lightly buttered and always healthy wheat or oat. Sliced apples or orange sections on the side. Myra watched over him to be sure he had his share. Great Health Food was a favorite theme and she never failed to remind him. Not nagging she defended, just from love.

Along with the coffee, they poured over the newspaper. Myra went right to the comics, then the coupons. She clipped away matching her comments of delight or frustration. Andre pulled out the sports and the editorial page. He needed to keep up on the Red Sox as a faithful member of "Red Sox Nation" and the Patriots in the fall. On to the Celtics and Bruins in the winter. Even if you weren't an avid fan, New Hampshire business people got a whole lot more successful if they could be at ease with the latest stars and the New England sports history – from Ted Williams to the Yaz,Quarterbacks Drew Bledsoe and Doug Flutie and his famous *Hail Mary* touchdown. You'd better remember the great Lakers-Celtics years, Magic Johnson vs Larry Bird and Bill Russell. You think Andy down at Best Cars doesn't know the hockey heroics of Bobby Orr and Phil Esposito? Course he does.

~ ~ ~

Andre read the editorials and letters to the editor with

a great thirst for what people are thinking out there. Myra listened to his can-you believe-this reactions with eternal patience. When her husband reached his weekly, these-guys-are so-pathetic-and-I-just-may-write – She had her line on cue, "Now Andre, you've got enough on your plate with the store. Not enough on it? I'll cook you another round. Scrambled or fried?"

After a fill of delicious breakfast, the coupons secured and the news properly sputtered about, Andre said, "Leave those dishes for us later. Come sit for another cup of your great coffee. I have some serious plans to share." That's when the topic of gun sales at the store eased itself closer to a plan. Andre finished his presentation with, "So then, you are agreed to have some trusted locals come in for a special breakfast and a discussion, to ease your mind? Let's hear how folks feel."

Myra was not an easy sell. Her final words were, "Ease my mind – or maybe push me to dig my heels in. But having Jed and Marnie – and Ray and Doc Ambrose in for my Sunday breakfast, that's just a fine idea. And Lionel, he stays quiet. Will be good for him. Nice folks and can't hurt business, however we decide. The store from the start has always kind of been theirs, the townspeople, as much as ours."

The following Sunday five locals who had strong feelings about guns were invited in to help Andre and Myra to come to their decision: to stock guns and ammunition in the store. They also came for the delicious breakfast. Myra's reputation for being a great cook was widely known in town. After the omelets, the crisp bacon, toast with homemade strawberry jelly and the coffee, the dishes were cleared, they fell into the discussion.

Around the table were Jed "Bull" Trussone, a giant of a man still trying to hold on to his dairy farm. He was known around as "Bull" for his power and size though he said it was because the cows were impressed by the name. He always added that "They're all girls, you know." Guns on the farm were as common as pitchforks for the hay. Then there was Ray Spencer who owned Spencer's Insurance – "We Cover It All." When he could get away, deer hunting season was at the top of his list. Did he also keep a revolver in his desk drawer. You bet! Ray was well known for a favorite line,"When I get to Heaven, St Peter may ask me, 'Hold on there, Ray. Are you packin?' "

Marnie Brodeur was there as a good friend and customer and known to be a crack shot. Her face was pallid and voice rough from smoking, but she was nobody to mess with. Lionel Durand was a Vietnam vet who had seen it all. He had special reverence in town for his service. And of course Dr. Evan Ambrose had to be there. To have a real discussion, they needed his strong antigun views. The doctor did his early years in city emergency wards. There was a second pot of coffee waiting. It would be a lengthy discussion. Way beyond the issue, this group had lasting respect for Andre and Myra.

Andre opened. He folded his hands on the table and began, with a chuckle, "As host I get to have even more than my say. Naturally Myra will have hers, especially since she put out that great breakfast." Nods and amens all around. "As the only hardware store in Helios and all that my father and grandfather did in its history, you know I want to go in a new direction. I intend to stock guns and ammunition.

Naturally, we will need to meet some complicated state and federal regs involved with the right to sell and the right to buy." He sipped his coffee letting the words sink in. "You don't just say, 'Okay Joe, here's a nice Smith 'n Wesson. Like that Glock? Well just hand me over the cash and take er away.' For responsible buyers owning a gun can be a real need – and certainly a right. If locals know any of the amendments – they sure know that Second one. But in the wrong hands – Well, Doc Ambrose will get his say here."

Myra began with a light touch, "Listen well and maybe you'll get to come another Sunday along down the calendar. Nice group." She moved to the serious, "Of course I am in favor of deer hunting season. Aside from the sport or the venison, I did some research. I know how to use a computer. We would be in real trouble at the store without our nice PC. I found out that probably the deer season is actually too short." She reached for a printout from her serving table. She went on, "There are over – let's see – over 1.25 million vehicle crashes with deer per year in this country. Some 150 deaths – 10,000 injuries and insurance payouts of over 3 billion. And here is another thing –"

Ray Spencer jumped in, "That's a damn tough concern for my insurance business. You know some out there actually say, 'If you see a deer in the road – don't swerve – try for a direct hit. Cars can be repaired and your airbag will protect you.' For certain, as Myra's facts said, the deer population and crashes are out of control." He paused and shook his head. "Also, we all know that deer can carry ticks and spread to humans causing that awful Lyme Disease. For insurance rates and for safety though, can't say I support that don't swerve advice. But teaching our sons and daughters, the skill and the pleasure of hunting, I am all in for that. For the deer population, there needs to be control and somehow keep it humane."

Ray stirred in his chair. He had more to say. "In my business, well, in American life – can you believe it, gun suicide is more common now than criminal killing. Over twenty thousand a year. Having a gun in the home can be – sometimes it – I am sure you get the point here."

Doctor Ambrose slid his cup to the side. He said, "Down in city Emergency a gun suicide that was – well sometimes it can end in a wound, a terrible one. Then when we work to save that person, what will be their reaction as they recover – incredible relief, distress, sometimes even resentful anger. We could be here hours on that troubling topic. To the point of guns in general though. We didn't see hunting accidents very often."

Doc Ambrose paused to get it right. As the best primary doctor in town – actually one of only three – locals fixed on his every word. He went on, "Like all big cities, Boston hospitals have a heavy run of gun emergencies – both the criminal kind and the police protection kind. Thank the Lord for the police. Here in small-town Helios, I hope I never experience again one like this one in the city, 'Dear God, I was sure my husband had that gun locked up. My son – my lovely dear son' – - Seeing those grieving parents. Trying to be a doctor while reaching out for their pain. The father hanging his head. The mother weeping unconsolably. These are memories that haunt me."

They were all hushed on that reality realized all too often. The weapon that was not locked. The gun that they were sure wasn't loaded. A child innocently bringing one to school. Quietly, Andre said, "Doc, we all dread these tragedies but the owners – they have to be responsible. Like teaching your kids that the family car can be lethal too if not used properly. The saying has some truth to it. Guns don't kill people. People kill people."

Myra stared out the window where clouds had eased past the morning sun. She said, "But that's it, Andre. I dread that it would be our people."

"They won't be our people Myra. You want Nelson down at Sunrise Chevy to be responsible if they choose to drive drunk and kill someone in a car they bought from him?" He held up his Sunday paper. "I admit the whole thing does get mighty complicated. Look at this article. There's talk of letting college kids carry guns on campus. Protection against lunatic shooters and intruders looking for easy property in dorms and for what they think is – well, lots of vulnerable and trusting women on every campus. Or, the other tragedy. Maybe they'll shoot a professor they hate right in front of the class. Maybe an armed student would become a hero."

"We don't choose the word lunatic anymore but the point is there. Dr. Ambrose ran his finger over the table as if noting a number. He said, "Mental health support for people who are in desperate need is a major concern in this country. And surely anyone who has a history of these needs should be checked with extreme care if they want to purchase a gun. It's part of the debate all the way to Congress."

~ ~ ~

Jed shook his head and said, "The Doc always brings us to some real serious thinking, that's for certain. He wiped his hands with the soft cloth napkin. Myra had put out the best settings for company. He pushed his plate aside and came back to life as he experienced it. "With the cows ready real early, I gotta say, don't get a breakfast like that too often. Myra, maybe you and Andre shoulda opened a restaurant instead." There were more nods of approval. The moment brought relief from the sadness and the reality they had just heard from the doctor. Jed went on, "Helios is not Boston. Yes, there are home accidents and some real domestic violence. No killing that I know of. There's always a 'yet' to everything, I suppose. Remember too that for a small town, we do have maybe more of our share of hunting accidents. Some of these tourist-hunters in deer season – more stupid than skilled." He paused for a can-ya-believe-this look. "For sure, in season I hear shots not far from my herd. Probably cases known somewheres of some poor cow or your dog out in the field getting blasted. Anything that moves. Definitely not the fault of a gun."

Another one of Ray's vigorous nods. He said, "Hard to believe but some of the completely irresponsible ones think a hunting trip is a time for a case of beer too. It's one thing to have beer on your boat for fishing – with a sober boat driver. But out there with a rifle – there's sure no reeling the shot back in." Ray was a talker. Some in town said they had more insurance than they needed – Ray had talked them into into it. But most felt it was good to support the locals. Ray went on to another topic, "It's my business to know risk – maybe even of disaster. Do you know that hundreds of guns are brought into lines at airports in luggage. Confiscated by security. The typical excuses, 'Gee, I just plain forgot – or my girlfriend packed my bag.' That whole airport security is such a huge issue."

Marnie found it was time for her to add. "Here's my two cents. I live at the end of a quiet street down there on Forester. My kids are grown and off, and Ted, he's gone on sales pretty often. Yes, I got me one of those nice revolvers ready in my night stand. I won't need the multiple rounds, I'm sure. One between the eyes should do the job." She added, "Chief Denton knows me. He knows my respect for safety. And he's seen me shoot at field targets. He'd know the truth."

~ ~ ~

Andre nodded his approval. "We are so fortunate to have the Chief. He'd do the right thing whoever's involved. We got in New Hampshire the Castle Law and Stand Your Ground. Someone threatens you with deadly harm – protect your castle – you can legally shoot an intruder with what seems to be deadly threat. Now Stand Your Ground you can defend with a gun anywhere. Gets very touchy with how to interpret though. Consider this scene. Guy knocks on your door. He's surly and maybe seems threatening. Reaches in his pocket. – You shoot him."

Myra picked up the story, "I know the rest of that one. It was his cellphone. Real tough one to lay the right blame."

Marnie extended her finger and fired off a fantasy shot. "Well if he's trespassin in my home – won't be any doubt about the blame!" She paused and eased into a more softened tone. "Ray spoke about this before. I have a personal tragedy – a suicide with a gun. Right in my family. A cousin over in Montpelier. I should say, *had* a cousin. Younger than me of course. So many problems, in and out of mental support care. He took his gun one night. Probably too easy, I guess." She put her hand to her face. She struggled on, " Truth is he surely would have found some other way. Poor soul. Whole family was devastated."

They all turned to Lionel who had kept his usual quiet. They knew there were many horrors he had never told, not even to Renee, his wife, or to his two sons. They took a family trip to DC every year to pay their respects at The Vietnam Veterans Memorial. Helios had three names on The Wall – three of that horrendous number of heroes – over fifty-eight thousand of them. There was silence again.

Lionel stood, no mistaking his military posture. His voice was deep and solemn. "You all know that guns in war are not what we are talking about here. If you have not been there, you can't really know. When the brave patriots fought in our Revolution, guns saved many lives, sometimes the lives of young boys fighting beside their fathers. And they helped win our precious independence – and the rights we have. Then the Civil War brought us the tragedy of brother shooting brother. All that is far beyond our hometown, but the truths are still there."

Lionel was back to instructor style again. Hands on the table, leaning directly to his class, he said, "The military are rigorously trained and know up close the issued personal weapon is their assigned and precious protector. Your weapon is like a part of you. It has to be." He sat back into his chair to bring home his final thought. "Here for our small village, anyone who purchases a gun and its ammunition should have the same rigorous instruction for safety and proper use. Also, it shocks me that an ordinary and untrained civilian can buy an assault rifle. An automatic that fires off repeated rounds per trigger pull.

Against police? Needed to shoot a deer? When you fire a gun – you must know this – It can be fun and exciting. It can be life saving. And it can end in tragedy."

Lionel dropped his head into his hands. Total silence. Finally he said. "This is very tough for me. You all know about military coming back to civilian life. The problems they bring back and the ones they find on return. Some can't stop re-living the trauma of the war violence. PTSD is a crisis in our country. Veterans know guns and it's terrible to say – too many use the gun to end the unbearable pain."

Myra let the silence linger but could not have the meeting end with that dark moment. "All right, my friends," she said, "don't think you're going to just leave this clutter for me and Andre. Grab a dish and a cup and head for the counter. Then we're all going out to see my geraniums. And yes, even my husband's attempt to be a farmer and grow tomatoes. He loves a delicious b.l.t. and more so – if the "t" is his very own." Andre always needed the last word so of course it was one of his classics. Pointing to Myra he chirped, "Take my wife – please" But as the guests filed away, Myra managed to still win over the last word, "When we was in school, Andre got pushed around because he didn't play hockey – you know – what – a French Canadian and all – so he got by being the class jokester. Thanks to the Marx Brothers and good ol Henny Youngman. She winked and said to Lionel, Any takers to that one?"

~ ~ ~

Patients chose Dr. Ambrose as their primary doctor partly because the choice was limited to just three in the town. Some saw him because it had always been that way in the family. Some because they liked his out-spoken

91

opinions and others avoided him for that. "Just get on with it" was their inner urge during visits. The doctor and his wife lived in a quiet white colonial with yellow shutters on what they found as the perfectly named street for a doctor – Hope Street. The name had many versions among the locals. Some as fun. Some as ridicule – that "rich folk" street.

Ernestine and her husband had a careful arrangement. One of them would be sure to be home at all times to cover any walk-in emergencies and phone calls. If it was the wife, she could contact the doctor quickly.

Ferdinand Laramie was the devoted school friend of Joey Driscoll because Joey had always been the one who stood up to the endless mocking, "Hey Ferdi-boy or" the Ferd-head" because a bully passionately seeks any easy target feature. His head did seem a bit large for his body. That he was a top student didn't help either when he showed them up in classes at Regional. The friends assured themselves that they were definitely "no druggies," but every kid knew about checking the parent's bathroom cabinet during house parties. Some kind of pills circulated around all the time. Regional High was called The Pharmacy by even the ones who enjoyed the rumors but not any available item. Much of it was required bragging.

Just to show they were both brainy guys and for the daring sense of it with something to prove, Joey and Ferdinand – FD to friends – dreamed up a scheme to break into Dr. Ambrose's home office and see if they could find any drugs. Make that steal any drugs. They chose a Friday, known to all as the doctor's day off for no hours. It was a cloudy afternoon with no western sun reflecting off his windows. They figured Fridays would likely be shopping day or a trip down to Lancaster or Whitefield for a lunch and a little away time. With their nobody home notion they both pushed mightily up on the window ledge bar. The older home latch creaked then suddenly popped. Joey nodded a, "Man, not even a sound yet." One at a time they eased through the window and landed softly on a colorful braided rug in what seemed to be a den. A couch and two chaise lounges faced a tv.

Joey peeked around the open doorframe and waved FD on, "Bet that's doc's office door right down the hall" he whispered behind his hand. Suddenly from the connecting room they were shocked – stopped cold. "Just what do you boys think are doing in here?" It wasn't a yell but a calm school principal kind of warning. This lady was clearly no one to challenge.

Officer Ainsworth came for this one. Boys home to parents and then eventually to Chief Denton. They learned with great reinforced regret about Dr. Ambrose and his wife and having that standing agreement to always have someone home. Even on any rare away vacation, his retired brother Jeff covered the house time. He always got a nice trip souvenir for his efforts, not coveted duty-free Jack Daniels though. Joey and FD, or naturally Ferdinand as the Chief addressed him, were sent on to Judge Sullivan. Scrubbing graphite off the town's fences was proper community service. The being seen and hooted at was the worst part. Ernestine had to refrain the doctor for not having himself a peek as well.

~ ~ ~

The sign in Lavalle's Hardware Store window in bold

print read: Coming Soon – A Full Selection of Guns & Ammo. Pictures of pistols and rifles surrounded the printed words. Shotgun shells and a pistol clip and holster finished the sign display. Willie Martin paused in front and examined the poster intently. He smiled and saluted the window. Aloud and with puffed up confidence, he said to nobody, "Well, now, won't have to travel for my ammo any more. Good work there, Andre. Count on me for a regular customer."

10

The days Jocelyn had her clean in the basement were Tracy's favorite. She fussed around the projects with a duster, she used Pledge to give the wood shelves a sheen. She cleaned the glass cases with Windex. She sat in the old school desk and wondered if it was the ones used by Grandmother Rousseau in her day. She had heard the tales of girls having their braids pulled by smart alecky boys sitting behind them. No hall lockers? Your desk was your locker. Every book, pencil case and lunch box would be in there. Your coat was in the coatroom, or was it called cloakroom? The kids didn't really wear cloaks, did they?

Tracy sensed the soft buzzing of the overhead fluorescent lights and the hum of the ever-faithful dehumidifier. She let her imagination be swept away into the fascination with all there was to learn. Now that she had heard the stories of Harry Kaiser The Collector, it all took on even stronger meaning. Logan told very little about his fantasy episodes. He did say though that they were very powerful images and forever moments between him and Harry. You had to be there. Tracy had slowly understood the respect Kurt and Logan had for Harry and Lillian, without ever knowing the true depth of their story. She wondered how much of it Jocelyn knew.

Moving On

For Tracy, the plan those mornings was the necessary cleaning. But she could tell that Jocelyn really was allowing time for her to explore and nourish her soul. It took probably an hour to clean and straighten, but she left her to be on her own until time for lunch. Tracy never rummaged as you might in your Aunt Tilly's dusty attic. She handled each item for the treasure it is. She would look at the famous clock in its corner and never know that amazing story either. She should ask Kurt if the 3:17 time it was stopped at had any meaning or just when the clock got tired and ran down. He passed it off as a run down. Unlike at a museum with the treasures under glass protection, most of these special collections were open to her careful and whimsical investigation.

On one of the many shelves, Harry had several books lined as a small library. She could see right away that Mr. Kaiser seemed to love Mark Twain. He had *Tom Sawyer, Huckleberry Finn, Roughing It,* and *Innocents Abroad.* She did not know the last two, but Ms. Harrigan had urged the juniors to read Huck Finn. She had said it was harder to read than Tom Sawyer but woven into the plot, there were themes filled with moral choices and truth. That subject always got Tracy's attention. She was a big fan of choices and the truth. She had tried to read Twain's famous novel but found the dialect very difficult and reluctantly gave up. Ms. Harrigan used the word "vernacular" which somehow stayed with her. She reminded the class that the French vernacular was not an obscure word at all. Some of the older French residents in Helios still held on to it.

As she ran the duster over the books, further in the line a very slim one caught her eye. It was obviously for young, beginning readers. It was titled *The Children's Own Readers*. She knew from research papers to look for publishing dates. Wow! 1920! – maybe really valuable. Jocelyn had said someday they would have to face up to having all these treasures re-appraised for increased insurance coverage from Harry's time and – and what? It would be a massive project with all the vast array collected and all the memories for Logan especially.

Tracy opened carefully to the Table of Contents of the child's reader. She found such stories as "The Elves and the Shoemaker" – "King Midas" – and "The First Thanksgiving." She remembered how in third grade Mrs. Sandersen had the kids dress as Pilgrims and Indians and recreate that special event. At the end, they even got to eat real turkey and corn on the cob. Tracy got to be the wife of the Chief. At the time she had begged for that role but now was mystified why it mattered so much to her. Somebody who really belonged maybe. Mom had helped to make the costume and had even dyed some old fabric to look like deerskin. She stored up those good Mom-memories. Then they had suddenly come to an end.

She knew the King Midas story about his craving for gold and being cursed eventually by the granted Golden Touch. He touched his daughter and – she too turned to gold. Tracy couldn't remember it, but she knew the tale must have a happy ending though, especially for really young kids. She promised to read it someday while she was in the basement. Can't leave the King and his daughter cursed like that. Fathers and daughters was the theme of her life.

She sat back on the bench by the books and thought

about Happy Endings. They should not be just for little kids' stories. She believed everybody should have one. Her Dad maybe was finding one. She hoped her mother too was finding hers wherever she may be. Getting out of this small town would become Tracy's mission to reach that goal. Also, along the way figuring out who she really was. Looks in her mirror at home left her pondering that question every day.

Jocelyn would soon call her up for lunch, so she looked around for one last dusting on some beckoning item. Next time she would vacuum. Jocelyn told Kurt that the basement was the cleanest room in the house. Actually Tracy had soon figured out that the dusting was more ritual than needed housework. Really an unspoken way for her to investigate the treasures and learn from them. What she found became a great topic for lunch on those days with Jocelyn. She knew some of Logan's experience there in that collection classroom. Now she would be the second one to learn there. It pleased her to think of following him. From her impressions, they both seemed sort of out of the mainstream in their high school time. And look how far he has gone.

~ ~ ~

Way off in the corner was a quiet spot she had hardly noticed because there were no shelves at all. She wondered why it seemed so unused. Moving closer, she noticed a small table and a dart board on the wall several feet in front of it. Instead of the regular target, it had a picture of a man. Not just any man. Junior History with Mr. Weston made sure everyone knew that man – Adolf Hitler – his famous mustache with the black hair slicked right on to the forehead. Mr. Weston had said they would absolutely get to

World War II this year. He was frustrated that students didn't know much at all about modern American history. Well everyone knew that Hitler was a really bad guy. FDR – Harry Truman – huh? Lincoln and Washington they knew. Eisenhower and General Patton from the movies. And Eisenhower was a president too – right? She knew that they were lucky to have a great teacher like Mr. Weston. If you also had a grampa to visit to tell his first-hand war stories, that would be extra nice.

Moving closer to the board, Tracy could see that Adolf had a few pinprick holes the darts had made by someone throwing them with obvious skill. Good shots! One right in the middle of his chin and two into the mustache. She ran her hand over the famous face. She remembered the word "infamous." That word was more like how a villain like him should be described. Tracy was excited by this new investigative style she was refining. On the table were coasters no doubt for the players. She wondered what they would drink. If Mr. Kaiser had service buddies in for the visit, for certain something stronger than lemonade.

In the middle of the table there was a wicker basket. Of course – it held the darts.

Some with red feathers, some blue. The smooth shafts ended in the gray metal points ready for the throwing. Why not! That's what they're here for. She carefully selected a red-feathered dart. A point test on her finger found it still sharp and ready to go. Tracy had never played the dart game in her life, but she was a fair badminton player in gym, and she had that nice overhand motion. She held the dart in front of her just as she had seen in a movie bar scene. Aim – swish – thunk – right smack into the sheet rock wall

beside the target. Learn a new skill, dummy. Three shots
later she was at least hitting the the target. Hold steady in
front – aim – and – yes! – right in that villain's nose. Tracy
strolled to the target and pulled the dart out with the grace
of a new champion. In the bar scene there was always much
hooting and clinking of glasses from the winners – and
friendly cursing from the losers.

As she moved back to the table, a strange new
excitement tingled through her whole body. Sudden
dizziness forced her to put her hand out to the wall for
balance. Then it struck her – why not the real thing for this
Mr. Hitler. She looked back for the shelf with the gun
display. Carefully she eased herself along between the
racks. The guns had both fascinated and unsettled her. At
the display, she found that one. She reached down slowly.
The barrel was cold and unyielding. She traced her finger
along its cold, gray metal. Tracy reached for the information
card and read it again: German Luger, designed by Georg F.
Luger in 1898. Used in WWI and by Nazi military and SS in
WWII. She eased the weapon away from its placement. It
was shockingly heavy in her hand, but the grip felt right.
The grip was a warm dark brown in contrast to the barrel.
With the weapon pointed downward to her side, she walked
back through the shelves. Surely it would have no bullets. It
wouldn't be actually loaded – would it? Again in front of the
target. He was still staring out – facing his world as if alive.
Smug. Evil. A German luger. How perfect for him. She
slowly raised the gun and sighted down the barrel. She
aimed it right at that ugly face –

"Tracy? Come on up for lunch." Jocelyn was at the top
of the stairs, right on time. She did not not hear any

response, so she moved down a few steps. The sight of Tracy standing there with a gun in her hand stunned her. "Tracy! What on earth!" Jocelyn rushed down to the floor level and crossed to her. She knew Harry would have never left his collection guns loaded. But always be careful. She reached out and slowly eased the weapon out of her hand. She was in a daze, still staring at the target.

"Tracy! You need to focus! Harry's guns are not toys. I am shocked you would ever touch one. Stay right with me. We are going to put this weapon back where you found it." Back at the display, Jocelyn placed the gun into its velvet case. She moved Tracy beside her, closer to see. She said, "Just as the card notes, this is a famous German Luger pistol. There, that flat, black piece beside the holster – that's the magazine." She held it up. "See, empty. No bullets in it. Tracy, I know guns. My dad made sure of that. I checked, none in the chamber either. Of course these guns are not loaded. Harry was a careful man." She grasped Tracy by the shoulders and walked her back to the dart target.

Right in front of the photo of Hitler, she said, "Okay now, you need a history lesson here. That man was evil – a sick tyrant. He knew that controlling young people – kids your age and even younger – would be the key for his future – his wild power fantasies. Be every day thrilled that you have the total chance to be free of any control like that. To make your own choices. You don't need to shoot him. Great American heroes took care of that sick dream – with stunning bravery."

Tracy looked down and managed to say, "So sorry, Jocelyn ... I just don't know why I – "

Jocelyn could see that she should tone it down. She

said, "Logan gave Kurt and me a good walk-around down here before he went off to college. He knew about the Hitler target, but Harry never made it a learning time. He said it seemed like it was a special private thing for Harry's buddies to come and talk war stories. And no doubt have a good competition with Hitler's face. Some of those friends may have known that fierce war up close." She paused with a softer look. "My Grandfather Simon was one of those those brave men. That awful Pacific part of the same war. He died as a POW."

In the kitchen, the clam chowder and the salad were eaten in quiet discomfort. Finally, Jocelyn broke the silence. No more Big-Sister. She became No-Nonsense Mom.

~ ~ ~

Tracy left for home on her bicycle with a clear certainty about the rules and the plain good sense down in the basement. And things about Hitler, not from a teacher. As she peddled along the images came with her ... what a great mom Jocelyn would be ... needed that good ripping ... and she sure gave it to me ... would my mom be strong like that ... me and my so sorry again ... She peddled faster.

Tracy pulled on to her Emmons Street. Her mother back then had taught her that Emmons was an easy one to remember – one of the few streets in Helios not named for trees. The Emmons family had a farm there, and when more of what Mom called "their clan" settled on nearby acreage, the dirt road to their places became Emmons Street. How do towns get street names, she sometimes wondered. Trees was the easy one. Mom was nice in those times and loved her. They had fun secrets. Mom was good at secrets.

Tracy didn't need a house key to carry around and forget in her school locker or lose out of her backpack. Her father had put in a keypad next to the garage door, and she easily remembered its code – 4/6/79 – her birthday. Her mother had said she was almost an April Fool's baby. That was funny when she was young. Not so much anymore.

Her father was out with Carol as was the pattern now. Out with Carol or Carol over to cook supper and watch tv – the three of them. When they were out, Tracy was by herself and liked it that way. In her room, she read by propping pillows against the bed backboard. She was all the way to the "D's" in the alphabet mystery series by the author Sue Grafton. The intricate plots kept her very involved. In this one, *D is for Deadbeat,* she once again related strongly to the main character, Kinsey Millhone. Tracy would tell anyone who would listen that Kinsey is a private investigator. That's a P.I. she would add casually. Tracy liked Kinsey's tough independence and the way she plunged into cases that seemed full of pitfalls. The Deadbeat in this book, among other crimes, is a bigamist. Tracy found it to be a strange word and even stranger situation. She wondered if Grafton would ever get all the way to the Z's. What on earth could be a Z title? Maybe "zero." She let her mind run on to how there would be zero clues to murders discovered only by KM's case solving skills. The series structure was just right for her. She felt she needed structure in her life.

Jocelyn had ended the afternoon assuring her that the Hitler dart board incident was over, and she should count on vacuuming down in the collection when that day came around again. Tomorrow they would pick cucumbers – if the woodchucks hadn't beat them to it. She was having a great summer – indoors with the house chores. Outside with the flowers and vegetables, sometimes even staying on for supper with Kurt there too. He always had good stories about somebody's car or truck at the shop and how careless they were to let the tire treads wear down so far. Tires and brakes – "Those are the biggies for safety," he would say. Sometimes he would tell about how the Kaisers had turned their lives around – his and Logan's. Tracy had seen the snowmobile in the barn covered with its blue tarp, but Jocelyn had told her best not ask about it.

~ ~ ~

After their supper and in the relaxed living room time, Jocelyn told Kurt in detail the serious dart board lesson she had given Tracy, especially about the gun display. "You know," Jocelyn said, "it seemed then like Tracy actually – I can't say liked it – the scolding I gave her – but she accepted it with many 'so-sorries' and head nods. Not at all typical these days. I hear from friends who have teen daughters that confronting toe-to-toe is pretty common. Daughter defiance versus Mom standing her ground. Tracy showed none of that adolescent push for independence."

"I'm sure no school counselor, but my brother and I know a few things about parents and being without them. Logan for certain." He leaned forward in the "Dee rocker" and said, "Tracy has had no mother for too many years. You are filling a real need, way beyond giving her a nice part time job."

"That means so much to me. For you to say it. Having Tracy with us, the good and the inevitable bad, is giving me a real sense of – well call it, reassurance – that maybe someday I can do the most challenging job there is – having a daughter of our own. Or son of course." She looked to see Kurt's reaction. The slight smile and the eyes were right. She pushed on. "A son would be nice for you, and either way an Uncle Logan would be just right for him. She took a pose. "Now then Kyle, you and I will drive down to Hanover and see the Dartmouth campus. Some great changes since I was there in '02." She did a good Logan.

Kurt laughed and gave her a "Bravo." He said, "And yes, by us staying poor, son Kyle can get a nice scholarship. Course he'll need better high school grades than I ever got. Or maybe he'd get one for baseball. I can certainly catch a kid's best fastball out back early evenings. Well, we'll need to buy new gloves. Mine would be pretty ratty and old for his power zips." Kurt sat back and pleased himself with the images. His time with Jocelyn had made him much more likely to talk seriously about the feelings he had kept carefully guarded for years. He went on, "The reality for kids – there is so much challenge these days. Too many decisions. Think about it, teens now with their own cars and ways to have money. And what teachers may say versus what each parent believes is right. The old New Hampshire *Live Free or Die* must give the history teachers some lively material." He smiled and added, "But there's always hope – look at Logan with his up and down life situation. Uh, maybe I should say 'down n up.' "

Jocelyn crossed to behind his chair and hugged her husband's shoulders. "And a thousand blessings to you. You've already been a parent. Yes, life for all of us can be so complicated and – Her sentence was cut short by the phone. Kurt went to the kitchen to answer. From the living room,

Jocelyn could catch pieces of his responses, but they gave no clue to the caller. She heard him say things like, "You have ta be kidding." and, "Seriously – you expect us to do that." Then his tone became quieter. She prayed that there was not something awful. Oh no, not with Tracy. Or God forbid – Logan.

Kurt came back into the room and sat. He said, "First I need to tell you, it was not bad news. I know you and your loved ones. You will never guess in a ten tries who I just talked with."

"Thank you for the no bad news part. You do know me. So then – who was it!"

"It was – my old classmate, uh, classmate and – whatever – Acel – Remy LeClaire's nephew." Kurt got up and from the kitchen and brought back refills of ice tea for them both. He went on, "It Seems Acel has finally got his life together way beyond what we last knew of him. He's got a job in Marietta, Georgia, of all places. From his lumber yard skills, he has gone on to some heavy equipment operation for construction sites. He did fork lift here and says he's got a future with this company. He's even in the required union. He's got a girlfriend and they are going to be married. Well, what can I say, she's pregnant already."

Jocelyn held her glass to the lamp light and watched the lemon float. She said, "So I still don't get it, Kurt. Why call you of all people. Not the best of old buddies ever."

"Oh brace yourself for this part. His Uncle Remy has died in prison."

Jocelyn gasped and struggled for the right words, "I suppose – yes – we knew this was coming. But it's especially sad. His life was such a tragedy in many ways. And to die in there. When we visited and then later Logan's visit – Remy as much as well – was resigned to his death – hospital time and all the signs. His cough with us was just awful. I don't think he was out of his sixties even. Very hard to tell. It is very sad to hear this news, but I'm not surprised. – There must have been more to this strange call, wasn't there? Go on."

"Oh yes, there is more." Kurt then told the full conversation about Acel's appeal for support. About the difficulty correctional officials had tracking him down and Acel needing to come for legal papers, an inquest and a burial. "He told me he is not going to do a service. He said, 'Really, who would come?' There is no estate to settle since Remy had signed over the property to him, and he had then sold it on to the county."

Kurt gave her time to let it all sink in. Then on to the essentials, "So here is our part. Acel pleaded with me, for us, to attend the burial with him. He's got no one here anymore. His Aunt Trudy has passed on. No one left in that family line but him. He said it would depress him to be alone. His girlfriend wants to go with him, but he said she really should not travel. Understandable certainly. She is pregnant and having bad mornings. Also, somehow he thinks we need a kind of end to the Remy story ourselves. That troublesome word 'closure.'"

Jocelyn did not hesitate a moment. She said, "Of course we'll do this.

Think of all the good that has come our way. We need to do this for both Remy and for help to Acel – a man who is trying to finally do good things with his life. Remember how Lillian ended that letter to Remy." She crossed to her desk and took out the letter's copy they had saved so carefully. With it carrying such a turning point in their lives, she had read the letter over many times. Here it took on a new and strange circumstance. She read the closing lines aloud:

> *I apologize for any discomfort I may be causing you. Perhaps you will come to accept that this is best for you as well. Slicing off some of that land for whatever you might plan then my selling to others -- it probably would not be comfortable for anyone.*
>
> *Dare I say to you, make good use of your time. I am dedicated to that goal in whatever years God may grant me.*
>
> *Sincerely, Lillian Kaiser*

Kurt walked to the window and looked out in the fading sunset to all that land. Turning back to Jocelyn he said, "Well dear Lillian, we now know how troubled neighbor Remy took that message. Rest in peace, you are still among us."

11

Before the grand opening for the gun sales at the hardware, Andre paid a safe courtesy call to Chief Denton at the station. He knew that the chief knew all the real details and all the gossip. If he had a reason to see Dr. Ambrose, he may have heard those concerns too. Myra had reminded him that his visit would be more than courtesy, that anytime they saw the chief, most likely it would be about guns.

The station was the sharpest new building in town – brick front, classic but modest white pillars at the entrance, a handicap ramp to handsome glass doors. Chief had given a strong testimony at the town board meeting even showing a video of the old wooden building and the cramped office space. He discreetly avoided the description "fire trap."

The board members fully knew they had postponed this pressing decision for too long. Costs and taxes, always the taxes. The basement jail showed up in the pictures as a shameful place even for overnight drunks. Chief had gotten a ripple of laughter when he tossed off a line about a Turkish Prison. In front of a full house of eager townsfolk, The Board voted the funding and the town unanimously approved it. Getting any New Hampshire small towner to take on a tax increase was famously difficult. That license tag logo was always in their minds. Most folks understood that famous line had to do with gun freedom, motorcycle helmets and personal rights, but taxes fit sometimes too.

When Andre came into the office, the chief stood up from his desk. It was always impressive to see what a six-foot three ex-Marine could still look like at his mid-forties. Pressed pants, shined shoes. Weapon holster at his belt with what Andre knew protruding out was the butt of a police-issue Glock. Chief didn't yet show much receding to that salt and pepper hair.

As Andre accepted the invite to sit, he looked around the office and said, "My first time in the new station, Chief. Missed your first-day open house, but I saw the ribbon cut. Big crowd came in support. I had to get back to the store, you know. Us townsfolk sure did the right thing. You and your Officer Ainsworth, well I know him as Billy of course, well, you have definitely earned these fine, new quarters."

Andre was nervous and knew probably he was saying too much. He hoped it didn't show, but he plunged right on with a little joke, "I spect traffic tickets paid for a good part of this, getting them summer tourists on their way to the lakes. Right , Chief?" He could see the chief was unmoved, but he chattered on, "Well probably its them Massachusetts drivers. We're all happy to see them help out with a fine or two. I drove around Boston once. Just once, mind you."

The Chief kept professional, he was not the easy remember-them-good-ol-days type, but he did get up to pour Andre a nice cup of hot coffee. Andre thought about some line featuring cops and donuts. That notion quickly passed.

"So Andre, what can I help you with this morning?" His

uniformed assistant cracked opened the door a crack and gave a hand sign for a phone call. He waved her off. Andre saw this short scene and was quietly pleased that the chief was choosing him over a call. The chief took a full swallow of his coffee and said, "I hear your grand opening for the gun sales is this week. LaValle's is entering new territory, and we are all for it. Why help out city gun stores? They will survive this competition, I'm sure."

"Yes, sir. That's why I'm here. More than any profit for our store, I think the locals will be very happy not to have to drive off for their gun needs. The real thing is this, I expect you know I have met all the regulations and I, that is me and Myra, just wanted to say that we will let you know if any weird out-of-towner becomes a customer. Unless the background check kicks out something – we gotta sell what they want ta buy. Right? And course we will want to."

"Andre, one of things about Helios, all small towns I suspect, there is a busy network. Any strange type that stops at the diner for instance – well, you know all about that. LaValle's has a great reputation going back to the family founders of the business. No one is getting by you and certainly not Myra. Actually we do have a couple of strange types right here in town. Isolated guys with no friends, always hanging around, changing jobs, trying to test the local speed limits. I believe we know our people."

Andre put his foot in it again. "Well Chief, guess you won't have to promote any buy-back gun program here. No gangs like the cities."

"I am happy to say we haven't had much criminal use of guns. We intend to keep it that way. Sure there is drugs, mostly marijuana. You'd be surprised the quiet use even some in homes of our upper class and summer renters for certain. Not in the park when we hear about it. Way too much prescription theft by kids partying in somebody's house. Wouldn't you think parents have gotten on to that by now."

The chief could see his phone lights were letting him know the day was in start mode already. But he went on with a voice that showed a real need to say it,"Our worse calls are the 911's from some wife or girlfriend, getting beaten up, even, so help me, a child. Domestic violence especially when employment is down or at the Christmas holiday time. A very sad pattern."

Andre understood that he had used his time. He drained his cup and said, "In the police shows on TV, they always fuss about lousy coffee. This was hot and like the real thing." He put his cup down carefully. "Uh, there is one more – well I need to tell Myra I said it. We were at Harry Kaiser's service back then – along with half the town it seemed. We thought you spoke so well. That story about the school prank with your father and Harry – it gave some relief to everyone."

The Chief nodded appreciation and stood. Andre knew the conversation was concluding but Chief added, "Harry was a good man for certain. I'm glad that your wife had that comment sent along to me. Thanks for that and for coming in Andre. Best of luck to you. We always like to be with the good guys."

When Andre exited to the Main Street sidewalk, the clouds in the south were knitting together into a grey blanket, and the first drops dampened his shirt. He thought – okay if it rains for our opening – - them good hardware locals won't mind a bit – no ponchos up here and no city umbrellas. He never missed the fun of calling the ponchos "city slickers." Myra had tried at times to explain the way of puns, but he always waved it off. He walked back to his store in fine comfort about his meeting with Chief and the prospects.

~ ~ ~

The sign in Lavalle's Hardware Store window in bold print read: TODAY – Come in to see >>> A Full Selection of Guns & Ammo. Pictures of pistols and rifles surrounded the printed words. Shotgun shells and a pistol clip and holster finished the sign display. Willie Martin paused in front and examined the poster intently. He smiled and saluted the window. Aloud and with puffed up confidence, he said to nobody, "Well, now, won't have to travel for my ammo any more. Good work there, Andre. Count on me for a regular customer."

~ ~ ~

The Grand Opening. Andre Lavalle was manning his new gun and ammo displays in fine style. He had known guns all his life and in preparation had put hours into current research and salesperson visits. Along the back wall were handsome shotguns for garden-raiding woodchucks, for skeet and trap shooting and for home defense. For deer season he featured Remington rifles and Browning as a more affordable price range than expensive Winchesters that run to multiple thousands. And yes, even AR-15 rifles with scopes for range and target practice and vets who knew their proper use. These weapons were a continuing political controversy with the NRA ever vigilant. If the pressure for restrictions gained a momentum of support, Andre knew that knew gun sales and ammunition for owners would skyrocket. The glass cases were sparkling with the pistol choices. There were Smith & Wesson revolvers and pistols. Andre featured S&W as a US manufacturer with a history back to the Civil War and the wild west. Their headquarters in nearby Springfield, Mass made it an easy choice.

He had the famous Sig Sauer guns, origin Switzerland, now manufactured in his home state south in Exeter and with a training school in Epping. Even Myra had to agree that if the Swiss watch was so great – why not their guns. And now in convenient NH. Andre had pamphlets about the training school right on the counter.

Then of course there was the world famous Glock and its Austrian founding and lively history. First controversial and even mocked as a "plastic gun." Then with mushrooming sales the concern for risky airport passage. It went on to become the standard for police all over the country – and a best seller for civilian use. At LaValle's you could spend from $300 to $3,000 and like cars, watch for the next models. Andre stocked holsters in stunning black or brown leather, backpacks, slings and pouches in khaki or the ever-popular camo.

Myra had to admit that the fanfare was exciting and any new profits would be welcomed. One of the best parts for her was seeing how excited Andre was the in this new role. It pleased her no end to see him as the Ring Master. Maybe they should put in gun-fan magazines too. Andre told her that they are called "gunnies" and are a big seller – long time past when every barber shop featured just Field & Stream.

Eighteen men, some with young sons, and three women

were in line, Everyone was chattering and pointing to their favorites. As with fishermen, local gun history flourished with exaggerated stories. Overheard: "Ah Gary, you need this shotgun for your crazy cousin." – - "Hey, we can make up our own army right here in Helios. March on Concord." – "Come on Ziggy, tell us the real deer season stories like your fishing luck, oh ya, the one that got away." – "All right guys, how about letting ladies first. And then watch ya back." Dory tried for a wink but his bushy brows brought a weak attempt." No mistaking, it was a happy group. Back in among the minglers Willie Martin kept quietly to the side. He'd take his buying time to when things were not so lively. Too many onlookers today but the grand displays surely buzzed his desires.

~ ~ ~

Willie picked a cloudy day, so he wouldn't be looking right into the sun. He'd been to the range before of course, but somehow this day would be extra special. He carefully packed his range bag – safety glasses - check – padded ear muffs – check – trusty weapon, the Glock with bullets separate still in carton – empty clip – no holsters allowed – no concealed weapons. "Yes sir, Andre LaValle, your fine product will soon see the light of day, my new rounds will be whistling right to the target." He headed the Chevy north outside of town to the Sunrise Shooting Range. As he drove, his plan to someday use that gun on hated "certain people" flashed along in the miles with him. ... probably not kill em ... but sure n hell, supply a real scare... but then they would be able to identify ... could get complicated ... The intrigue was warm and welcoming as it churned in his brain.

There were no indoor ranges in the area at all, so

Moving On

Sunrise was a welcomed business for local gun lovers. It had been constructed in a vacant field fully out of the way of homes or farms. Bud Foster was an army vet with twenty years of service and enough retirement pay to follow a dream he'd had for years – to own and operate a gun range. He'd stress safety, teach skills and enjoy his faithful returnees. Day off for rainy days and then down to Florida escaping the rugged snow months. He thought "snowbird" was a perfect name for these timely retreats. Florida had indoor shooting ranges in many locations where he could keep up his own skills and shock the fellow shooters with his accuracy. Didn't take long to make friends. Safety rules bring courtesy too and maybe an invite for a drink. Always after, of course.

Willie parked along the line of vehicles, mostly pickups. Busy day. He liked that feeling of being "one of the boys." More and more women there too he had noted. He headed for the shop to pay the fee, be checked in and cautioned about rules though for him it was really routine. As he walked across the lot, he could hear the repeated sounds of the gunfire – a steady pow, pow. Though it was an outdoor range in rugged rural territory, there were no stones or trees to zing off a ricochet like in the movies. A carefully chosen grassy embankment absorbed the lead and it was not near any water for the bullet lead to leach into.

Bud was behind the counter and greeted Willie as a returnee who respected the rules. Nobody called him Bud. He was still "Sarge" or for the real vets, "Masasagent." You had to slide through the syllables as a sign that you'd been there. Twenty years in the U. S. Army, Honorable Discharge as a Master Sergeant, a rank demanding total respect and unyielding leadership skills. In the town Memorial Day parades, sharp in his uniform with the insignia stripes on his sleeve and array of service ribbons, Sergeant Foster barked the cadence to the marching vets. The unit always got patriotic salutes and rousing cheers from the locals lining the sidewalks. Kids waved their souvenir flags and tried to catch the pace and keep up along the sides.

Willie read yet again the safety rules posted: "No smoking. No horseplay. Visitors not allowed. Always wear ear and eye protection. Without the Range Officer's Signal - never move forward beyond the restriction lines. Cease Fire means Cease Fire!" Willie always thought those rules pretty unnecessary for him. Never smoked behind the school. That scruffy bunch would have kicked him out. Nobody ever invited him into horseplay. Roland Santois, known back at Regional as BigRS, led the smokers pack and was one of his worse tormentors. Maybe he should put him on his "better-watch-it list." And Willie certainly didn't "expect no visitors." He always had his protective gear – and – only a total fool would ever go out beyond the line. He was always alert for the Cease Fire and the Officer's signals.

Bud's son Jimmy was the Range Officer, all business. He came to Willie's lane position and equipment table. He unzipped and checked his bag. Yes, pistol pointed down range even in the bag. Clip empty and easily viewed when placed on the setup table.

Just as he planned, Willie fired off his standard fifty rounds. Could have done a hundred but ammo is not cheap. Glock performed like he knew it would. Perfect. When he went out with the other shooters to check his target each time, he told himself, "Not bad, not bad at all." That was his forgiving assessment anyway.

On his way out, he stopped again to chat with Sarge. Just being around such a confident guy made him feel good. Sarge said, "Got a minute for a story, Willie? One of my army buddies sent me an email. After discharge, he went on to his town National Guard. They go for the annual two weeks required duty training. At the fort firing range, some AWOL recruit was sleeping off a drinking bout the night before. Where's he sleep it off – in the bushes behind the range."

Willie even took off his cap to scratch his head on that bizarre choice. He said, "Guess I know the ending here, right Sarge?"

On his drive back home, Willie thought about the story and the recruit's incredible stupidity. Sarge had finished the story by saying that yes, indeed, a ricochet round went right through the guy's chest and cleanly out his back. Still half buzzed when they took him out on a stretcher. He was alive and maybe the wiser for another day. Probably sober for a while – oh, and a Discharge too of course. Sarge could tell a story. Willie knew that he'd made his mistakes as everyone does – but Stupid like that – hard to believe.

12

Tracy was looking forward to another special day – one more trip with Logan and Kristen. With summer winding down both were getting ready to return to college. Logan pushed for the chance to drive Kurt's new Dodge Ram again, this time to take Kristen back to Middlebury and a chance for Tracy to see a fine college campus. Now that Carol was in Dad's life, he was much more ready to find Tracy's decisions increasingly mature. Tracy was still Tracy, but Carol was giving Dad a definitely new outlook, and she found great comfort around Kristen and certainly with Jocelyn. Amy Saunders was her best friend at Regional, but she was off for the summer at tennis camp and with the time at the farm, the weeks went by. Amy's main goals were making the tennis team again and lining up the right boy for the Senior Prom in the spring. Tracy did not play tennis. Senior Prom? Months away and not a major item on her planning plate.

To use her time in the evening and to not be too churned up for tomorrow's trip, Tracy took a bike ride around the neighborhood. The sun was easing itself west to Vermont and clouds were gathering on the horizon. The sun chose one huge cloud to halo-ring itself with dazzling light. Emmons Street was classically middle class – ranch homes, some split levels – and further along easing itself into more upscale properties. She liked passing homes that had families enjoying the pleasant evening weather – teens dribbling basketballs on the driveway pavement in two-on-two hoops and yelling out "Yes!" for a great shot and smoke drifting up from barbecues in the back. Dogs bounding about, little kids splashing around in wading pools. She still had bad memories of how she had nearly ruined the last trip with Logan and Kristen. That pitiful scene on the Cannon Mountain walking trail, her being so sorry for herself. That day of all days.

No more "so-sorries" wishing her life was more like these seemingly perfect family scenes. Mr. Weston had another gem he told the class every year. Back in time, there were women in this one native village – and everyone of them had a seriously bent back, what in modern medical terms may be referred to as scoliosis. One day a wise woman realized that the strangeness of these bent backs was not their humble food or the air or the babies they carried – but the fact that they all swept the streets every morning bending over their short broomsticks. So voila! Longer broomsticks gave the women great relief and their daughters a new future. Mr Weston said the story is a longer version of – "Time to turn over a new leaf." Tracy was determined to rid herself of her emotional bad back. She would do her part to make this sendoff for Kristen a super one.

Early the next morning when Logan pulled into her driveway, Tracy could see he had already picked up Kristen. Of course. She popped out of the passenger seat and even at 7 A. M., Kristen was flashing her usual energy. "So there

Tracy, I see we're wearing our matching Middlebury tee shirts. Way ta go! Good start to our day"

Tracy found the second seat in the quad like a familiar campsite. Nice leather was just right and plenty of room. Just like the trip they had taken to the Franconia Notch. The rear seat was perfect for her as playing backup to these two high-confidence college students. Logan leaned over the seat and said, "Hope you noticed, same sweet set of wheels you were in for the other trip. Kurt's willing to lend it off to me again cause then he can take Jocelyn's grand Chrysler 300. Nice one-day trade off."

Kristen leaned back to add, "Had to have the pickup to transport my new prized possession – that glorious dorm room fridge in elegant black. It's back there in the truck bed all protected with a tarp. Freshman year I pretended I wouldn't need one. Not smart. A mini fridge is just great for days missing cafeteria, snacks or down time. Roommate Melissa shared hers, but that can, you know, get tricky"

Tracy turned to see through the rear window there were several bundles in the truck bed. She said, "See that, I've learned a vital thing about college life already." This time she passed on taking her protective easy out, "Probably will never need one though."

They sailed south along I-93 at never more than a touch over the speed limit – a speed ticket would be the end of any Ram 1500 for Logan. He knew that well. They reached Montpelier and found downtown a special place for lunch Kristen had discovered from last year with her parents' trip. La Brioche Bakery & Cafe. As they waited for the sandwiches and drank iced tea, Kristen said, "I'm going to be sure my roommate Melissa has lunch here some day. La

Brioche for French pastry. She's has already set on a French major and will have classes in that beautiful Le Chateau campus building. We'll be sure to see it. My roomy is from the Finger Lakes region of New York, famous for its wine. She hopes that a French major will be a big plus in wine importing." Kristen tried to assume a formal Melissa voice, "We will of course import the Bordeaux wines and export our very own Riesling and Pinot noir." Then in her casual good-ol-me again, "Don't you just love the elegant French names. With the French-Canadian around Helios, I should have been the French major. But I don't even like wine."

"Me neither" said Logan. I'll be twenty-one next year and could be a big-time legal guy in a bar. Not that a college campus would have any under-age drinking. Just never happens." No smirk needed.

"Of course not – underage drinking on campus? Actually, Middlebury is not a big party school. Kristen touched her forehead and added, "Clear heads required."

Tracy relished these exchanges but was alert to when her contributions weren't useful. As if anyway she would have some special insider information. She was not about to add that some really under-age kids at Regional found ways to get beer on the weekends. Kristen changed the subject. "The last time we were together, Tracy, at the ice cream stand, at I-Scream, we were coming back from that great trip to the Air Force recruiter. Very weird scene. That creep Willie Martin invited himself into our table – I hope you've not had anything more from him? Have you even seen him?"

"No but I'd sure know him if I did. All hot-shot camo and a jacket in summer. Black Chevy pickup. Something like really strange about him. You felt that too, right Kristen?"

"Oh yes. But you did tell your dad about it and most important, about the threat he made. I trust you did."

That was Kristen now in her serious tone. Tracy wanted, needed, her approval. She looked down and back up instantly, then the clearing of the throat, always her tel though she had never played poker in her life. She said, "Well uh, no actually, I didn't. Not yet anyway. That Willie said he and my father had, I remember he called it like 'a little incident.' But Dad has never said anything to me about any incident or Carol either, so, I let it drift hoping there was not much to it." She could not tell what Kristen thought of that answer as Logan was up settling the check. It would gnaw away at her, she was sure.

"Okay let's get on the road. It's not far from here." Always ready, Logan led the way. He said,"We'll go first to Kris' dorm and move her stuff in – and very carefully that new grand fridge. Then do a campus tour and be on our way back."

When they eased the truck through the campus gates, Tracy craned to take in as much as she could. Beautiful classic brick buildings, paved walks and bike paths, expanses of grass and manicured shrubs, no litter anywhere despite full summer sessions. As they pulled to a loading curb beside Kristen's dorm, Freshmen volunteers rushed out to help.

The three walked to the Center for the Arts building, and Tracy was overwhelmed at the stage and performance areas for music, dance and theater productions. She knew her repeated "Wows" were a bit lame, but it all left her so impressed. Kristen led them to a row and said, "Let's sit and I will give you a grand backstory. This school was founded way before the Civil War – 1800, not that long after our Revolution. One of the first in the country. Well there's Harvard years before that, of course.

"And not to overlook good ol Dartmouth." said Logan. We came in at 1769. Students are supposed to know these things. Tradition, tradition, tradition. Should I name some famous grads?" He nodded to Kristen. "Okay it's definitely your show."

Kristen went on to note that the foreign language majors at the school made it seem like the world was getting very small indeed. Everything from Chinese to Hebrew to Russian and Arabic and many more. She joked, "You name it, we got it. Maybe even Inuit if you want to study the history of the Eskimos. Here's one from Melissa that stuck in my brain. Just eighteen percent of Americans speak a second language. In Europe its fifty percent." She went on to brag a bit about the nearby Bread Loaf Campus where maybe she might make sometime the famous Writer's Conference with her English Lit major.

Logan added that between the two campuses, in the fall Vermont and New Hampshire pretty much locked up the reason for tourists to drive their roads – for the stunning fall foliage. They came to see those New England towns with white steepled churches surrounded by the brilliant colors in every photo. And ski resorts by the dozen in both states. Photo calendars were big sellers.

Back in front of Kristen's dorm again, they stood by the truck to say their goodbyes. Logan's parting words were, "Fill that fridge with all good stuff." Tracy tried to look away, but she watched for anything more than words. Possible kiss on the check or embrace. Not happening.

Tracy held tears, but she did receive Kristen's promise for a weekend visit back home. As they turned to the truck,Tracy never hesitated. She popped open the passenger side door and said,"Well, one good thing, now I get to ride shotgun." It made for a good-confidence wave.

Logan wanted to drive along a country road they had passed and maybe get a few photos. They had seen horses grazing behind white fences. From Kristen's father, he had stirred a photography interest and thought it could evolve to a part of his history major. A simple Nikon was all he could afford, small but it had some range.

Off Rt. 7 he found the side road again. The horses were still grazing in the field. They got out of the truck and walked quietly to the fence. There were just two, one a soft cream color all over, the other a rich brown with white markings down the forehead from the ears to the nose. The horses wandered up to the fence and leaned their heads over. But the fence was doubled no doubt to keep eager visitors from petting muzzles and offering food not approved but taken all too-readily.

Logan said, "I don't know a thing about horse breeds, never even rode one. But these two are beautiful. Stand by the fence, Tracy, for a picture shot." She struck a stiff pose, hands down beside her waist, head straight on, a forced smile. He waved at her and scoffed, "Come-on there you, not for a police a line-up. A nice yearbook candid. Hand on the the fence, face angled to the horses."

Back in the truck, he headed farther down the narrow road to find a safe turning spot. A ways along, there was a small pull-off clearing to the side. Just as Logan began to swing out for the full u-turn – Tracy jumped in her seat. Pointing ahead she blurted out, "Logan! Look up there on the hill! Smoke's pouring out of that house. That's sure no backyard barbecue!"

"Sure isn't! Not a trash pile either. Comin right from the roof! We're goin up there!" In seconds they bumped along into the rough driveway. By then the smoke on the roof was showing flames finding air and licking across the shingles. Logan shouted a take-charge command – "Tracy – Stay by the truck. Here's my phone. Call 911!" Logan raced across the porch to the front door – banging and yelling Fire! The door was not locked. It opened to a long darkened hallway. He ran on to the kitchen – yelling "Fire!" No one there. No one in adjacent living room either ... am I gonna do this ... he leaped up the hallway stairs two at a time ... first bedroom – nobody ... second bedroom ... the door was already hot ... he dropped to his knees and pushed in ... a woman was collapsed face down by the door ... a wet towel had slipped away to the floor ... she stretched her arm to reach for it ... the room was dark with thick, acrid smoke ...

Logan reached down and grabbed the woman under the arms. He kicked the door to full wide and pulled her out to the hall. She gasped for breath and coughed fitfully over and over. With great care, he pulled her along the hallway. He could see that she was clearly old and frail. Her grey hair hung loosely down to her blue nightgown. He put his face close to hers, "Can you walk? Can you do the stairs with my help?" Smoke was spewing out into the hall. "We gotta go!" With his arm around her shoulders, he half-walked, half-dragged the woman down the stairs through the door and across the porch. Now carefully down the steps and out to the front lawn.

Tracy rushed to them. Together they eased the woman to the ground. Face up, she was gasping and struggling to breathe, as was Logan. The fire was racing across the roof and sending flames shooting out of the opened top floor windows. Tracy remained incredibly calm. Now in her in-charge voice, she said, "I know CPR from Health class."

She slipped down to her knees beside the woman and looked to her chest. Her chest was moving though the breathing was very shallow. "Ma'am, can you hear me? My name is Tracy. I'm going to help you!" The woman exhaled one long breath and her chest didn't rise again. Tracy leaned down placing her ear to the woman's mouth. Nothing. She placed her thumb on the woman's chin opening her mouth as she tipped her head back. Tracy took a deep breath and exhaled two short quick breaths into the woman's mouth. She placed one hand on top of the other and found the center of the woman's chest. She pushed down and began counting to thirty before starting the process over again.

In the distance sirens were wailing as they swallowed up stretches of road. "They're coming!" Logan gasped out to Tracy between coughs. She didn't so much as look up at him. Her adrenaline had taken over.

Tires squealed as a white SUV wheeled onto the driveway, lights flashing. A man clutching a radio jumped out of the driver's seat. He shielded his hand against the sun and peered at the house. He swiftly made his radio report. "Vergennes Car One has arrived on scene, smoke and flame showing from second floor windows." Then he spotted

Logan, Tracy, and the woman on the ground and rushed to them. Logan first, kneeling beside him and placing a hand on his back he said,"How ya doin' son? I'm Chief Parker with Vergennes Fire. Is anyone else inside the building?"

Still struggling with coughs, Logan answered as he could, "I don't know sir. I was able to get this woman out – but that was it."

Chief moved to Tracy and the woman. He called back to Logan, "That's good work, son." Turning to Tracy, he said firmly,"I'll take over, you've done fine work here." Chief continued another thirty count of chest compressions before stopping and returning to his radio. "Start an ambulance, confirming two victims, one unresponsive and not breathing. Unknown if the house is clear."

The radio responded clearly – a woman's voice, "Copy, Car One arrived confirming a Ninety-nine, also confirming two victims and unknown if the house is clear."

Loud beeping came through the radio and it reported again, "Bristol Fire and Rescue, request for Ambulance, one Engine, and Truck 2 for assisting Vergennes on a confirmed Ninety-nine with two victims."

Then a sudden new voice came through the radio. "Go, go, go!" A fire Engine roared into the driveway with just the lights on, a hose sliding snake-like off the back and leading around the corner. The Engine pulled up near the house and five other men jumped out running covering all directions. The driver connected a smaller hose to the pump. One of the men from the back grabbed the other end of the hose and ran over to the Rig Officer. He was wearing a red hat instead of the standard yellow. It showed he was also Captain..

The Chief directed, "Grab me the First-In bag and the AED!" The man ran back to the Engine and opened a compartment full of bags of different colors. He grabbed the green one putting the strap over his shoulder. He held a small gray bag in his hand and dashed back. He opened the gray bag first, extracting a protected razor blade. He skillfully sliced an opening in the the woman's nightdress. Working around the Chief who was continuing the chest compressions – he removed paddles from the bag and carefully secured them to the woman's chest. The AED notified in auto,"Charging. Ready." Chief pulled his hands away and nodded to his partner, then pushed the red respond button. The defibrillator shocked the woman, causing her to arch her back. The Chief started chest compressions again as the machine recharged. His partner took the oxygen out of the green bag. The AED shocked the woman again. Then a welcome beeping – there was a heartbeat.

"Ma'am, can you hear me? I am Chief Parker with the Vergennes Fire Department. We're going to place an oxygen mask on you and get you help – okay?" She nodded weakly and they secured the mask. "Watch her," he directed. Chief stood and looked to Logan and assured him, "We're going to be certain you have help too."

Logan's cough had gradually subsided. He assured the Chief that he did not require hospital emergency care. As the ambulance pulled into the driveway, he signed the necessary papers to decline. Engine and Truck from Bristol FD arrived behind the ambulance. Their Backup went to instant action at the house which was still engulfed.

Sections of the roof had already caved in. The flames

roared high into the air. Two firefighters from Bristol's Truck grabbed a set of irons. One of them ran to the front door where the Vergennes firefighters waited with hose ready. The Bristol men rammed open the door and dove to the side. The Vergennes' fighters sprayed power-streams of water into the doorway. No flames on the first floor, but it was completely dark with swirling smoke. Bristol firefighters rushed to the back door with a hose at the ready.

The two teams worked together and fought their way to the bottom of the stairs. They could barely see the hose in their hands. One fighter yelled,"Grip that hose! No black hole!" They carefully inched up the stairs and battled the fire raging down the hallway. They sprayed the walls from the top to floor. "Knock down this fire!" Designated fighters pushed through the front door and became the search team. With fire extinguishers and pipe poles, they began the overhaul. They poked the ceilings and the walls, making certain that no fires may have been trapped inside.

The woman rescued from the burning bedroom was on her way to the hospital.. The Chief pulled Tracy and Logan aside and said, "You two are heroes. You saved that woman's life and at the risk of your own. It takes a special kind of bravery. You are in line for awards."

~ ~ ~

A week later, Logan and Tracy were at the Vergennes Fire Department, in the auditorium surrounded by the full company of firefighters. Kurt and Jocelyn, Tracy's dad and Carol and Kristen from college were there to share the amazing event. The Chief announced, "Today, we are here to honor two very brave persons for risking their own lives for strangers. So in this special ceremony, we present the medals of heroism and bravery to you, Logan, and to you, Tracy."

Both medals gold with the Maltese Cross and the words "honorary firefighter" printed on them were placed around their necks. The full fire company and the visitors stood and applauded. The Chief began to speak again, "We also have a third special guest here upon her request. The grateful woman who was rescued waved weakly from her wheelchair. She formed the words that said it all – "Thank you. Thank you."

~ ~ ~

Still glowing from the medal ceremony for Logan and Tracy, Kurt and Jocelyn met Acel at the driveway leading up to his Uncle Remy's farm house. This would be a markedly different occasion. No long-lost-friend embraces, just polite handshakes. Acel shuffled his feet and said,"You two will never know how much I appreciate what you are doing for me today. I just couldn't face it alone." He pointed up to the farmhouse. "And look, the county has already completed work on his house and land I sold to them." Acel removed his hat and waved it toward the house showing complete amazement. "Look at that, will ya. New roof, shaker shingles in place of the old, half painted sides. Proper sidewalk, lawn mowed and shrubs trimmed. Uncle Remy – hard to tell if he'd like all this dressing up or, you know, hate it cause it would never be like his home to him."

They walked up to the porch and found yellow security tape across the entrance steps. Big sign: Riverside Coos County Park – Grand Celebration Coming Soon – Fun For All Ages – Coos County Board, Al Gradner, Commissioner.

Kurt said, "Pretty impressive, right? We've seen the

work trucks and have watched the progress for weeks now. The house has been converted into an information center and has exhibits as well."

"Yes, for different kinds of New Hampshire trees with bark and leaf samples, evergreen needles and like that." Jocelyn smiled and added, "Field trip planned for my eager church class already. We'll walk the trails through the trees and find some of nature's prizes. Amazing. We live among this beauty all our lives, and yet many of us can't tell much beyond a Christmas tree."

"Or want a tough one. I learned about this from Harry – a birch and its cousin, the poplar. Very similar look but some real differences." Kurt pointed to a fine birch with a double trunk near the house. But he let it go about the differences.

"What a great thing for the town. They're even bringing in a traveling carnival for the celebration night with fireworks for a finale." Jocelyn said,"See, back along the side of the house, the new exercise trail begins there and runs all the way to the river. It has workout stations all along it. Commissioner Gradner is a big fitness guy, so he's promised to be first to challenge the trail."

Kurt added,"Right, at a workout station you get to rest from jogging or walking while you do pull-ups on the bars. Me? I get my exercise at work and in our gardens."

Acel opened the door of the rental car and took out the box with Remy LeClair's ashes. It was no more than a small, simple chest. He said, "Let's walk down to the river edge for this. At least now with the remembering for him we're doing this morning – well the real remembering can be this wonderful park. Won't be any dedication to him naturally.

Everyone knows where he ended his life, but think now all the good comin from the place."

Acel held the box carefully as if fearing it would break. It was obvious to Kurt and Jocelyn that he was extremely nervous and awkward in this unfamiliar role. He had reasoned that the county surely would not object if the original owner of the land, Remy LeClair, had his ashes scattered on it by the river. When Acel had told Kurt and Jocelyn his plan, at first they were dismayed at the very thought of it. Remy in a parallel final resting place – just a short farmer's distance from dear Harry Kaiser – it bordered on sacrilege. It took considerable soul searching for them to accept. But they had agreed to be there for Acel, and finally they worked it through. They decided that since Logan had reached the confession and forgiveness part in his visit with Remy in the prison, somehow it seemed to be the right thing to do. What could be the reason to harbor bitterness on and on. And Acel seemed so – so nearly helpless with it all.

Acel opened the box and said in a low voice,"We could have, you know – at the river, in the water – but Uncle was surely a land guy. All his life. He will have a small marker in the town cemetery. It's the proper thing. He scattered the ashes. Helped by a gentle breeze, the ashes spread along the grassy field. He looked skyward at the drifting clouds, and did manage to say, "Well, Uncle, I do want you to rest in peace." With their heads bowed, Jocelyn and Kurt added their amens.

Back at home, after a quiet supper, Kurt and Jocelyn stayed at the table to sort out their feelings from the strange day. They tried to resolve their acceptance. Jocelyn broke the silence, "It is so difficult, Remy and all his anger, now his resting place is just a short way from Harry's. You know I am ashamed to say that before Acel left I wanted to – well, it would have been more unkind than is my way – but let him know that the flowers, the glads, that he and Remy stomped down are now back in wonderful full bloom."

Kurt nodded and said,"I've had some getting-even thoughts for these years as you know. But I'm at peace with it more now. It's good you didn't send Acel away with those parting shots. And him and his girlfriend having a baby and not wanting her to travel up way here from Georgia. You have to think he's done some serious changing." He slid back his chair and added, "Maybe we need to lighten up this discussion. What do ya think? It might have been better if Acel had done the ashes up at Lake Francis, you know, where Remy said he had tossed his rifle in to the fishes. They'd be together forever."

"Really Kurt, don't be putting any downers like that on the wonderful time we had there at the lake. That notion would have ruined it for me." She began to clear the supper dishes. She turned and said, "You want to lighten this up? Did I ever tell you that Mark Twain is one of my favorite authors and –

"Oh, oh, here we go."

"Twain had so much fun with *Huck Finn* and *Tom Sawyer*. And all the time sneaking in a few twitches to make the reader ponder a bit. In *Tom Sawyer,* the town has a funeral for the two boys thinking they had drowned in one of their adventures. Not actually drowned of course – what would he do with the rest of the novel? Hiding in the back of the church, the boys get to attend their own funeral.

There is much weeping and talk of how sweet these lads were. Of course then they have to come out of hiding and be loved again. And in equal parts soundly scolded." She placed dishes near the washer and went on. "My real point is – suppose Acel did have a service and Remy could hear all that was said about him."

"Now there's a scene. What should be done anyway at a service for a guy like him? Scramble to find some good things to say, or even be forced to – well, you know, downright exaggerate? Would Logan be chosen to say a few words? Ah the college boy, considering his history with ol Remy, that would be – "

"Yes, a test of character for both the speaker – and the deceased." She set off the dishwasher. I guess all said and done today, these whimsical thoughts may be good solace for us. There now Remy, all's well that ends well."

Kurt walked over to Jocelyn. He pulled her in close and whispered in her ear, "Even I know that one."

13

Tracy's friend Amy was back from tennis camp, and with school starting the week after Labor Day, they had much to talk over. Amy lived on Emmons Street too, her family in a white colonial farther along toward the high-end homes. An older brother Alfred was at UNH downstate. Amy always made the point that nobody should ever call him Alf. He'd heard it all through school, "Hey! It's Alf-Himself." Tracy assured her what they both knew well: take that easy one and run with it. Definitely one of the better ones. Didn't hurt that her brother was the captain of the baseball team. Amy was a perfect match for Tracy as the crucial tether that attached her to a bigger group, an envied "almost in" one. Amy had always just plowed ahead with connections while Tracy would have been barely noticed at all on her own. Her friend's repeated advice, "Ya gotta be more decisive, that's it, Tracy – be decisive."

"Yes, a good one. Oh those beloved vocab assignments. Tracy held up a gestured notebook. "I got em all from the homework and even my sentences ol Mr. Billings requires. But I always like hated it when he wanted us to read them out to the class. Remember that we had fun callin' them Billins Fillins."

Tracy's repeat in person of the now famous story about

the rescue at the house fire and the award presented to her and Logan changed all that "be decisive" topic. Amy had even heard the story away at camp and had raved about the rescue to everyone. It would make Tracy's return to school a whole new scene, they were sure.

Amy's father had two gigantic oak trees cut from the front of their lawn for more light and to his pleasure, not so many leaves to rake in the fall. He had the remaining stumps made nearly smooth to become matching seats close to the street and well away from the house. Good spot for a talk and to watch the passing scene. There were familiar neighbors who drove by and waved and Mrs. LaFlame who walked her pure white poodle with the name Fancy. Fancy was a purebred poodle with those long legs and that superior look. The girls thought the name to be "like way too much." Amy had fun accenting the dog's name as fahn-<u>say</u>. They never suggested it to the owner however.

Mr. Durand's English bulldog Rufus was great fun though. He visited them happily on his required Visit Route. Some days Rufus just plunked down on the grass next to the girls, stretched out with his rear legs spread in full-rest mode and refused to move. Mr. Durand would say that he's camped out near his two girlfriends. Amy's treats from her pocket likely encouraged the whole performance. The girls decided that if Rufus was a boy in fifth grade, he would soon be called Goofus or Doofus. It'd be just too easy.

On one visit while Mr. Durand waited for Rufus to have his full, proper visit, he asked the girls if they knew about the very famous bulldog Uga, the mascot of the University of Georgia football team. Amy may have known some of the fame, but they both played dumb to be sure Mr. Durand could enjoy telling the story. He said, "Oh there have been many Ugas over the years. Uga stands for U of GA. Clever, huh? The dogs even get a student I. D. and make a big appearance at the games, in uniform of course. Go Dawgs! And all that great rallying cry. You girls watch for a televised game this fall. Rufus and I are big fans when the dog appears, but he eventually gets bored with the regular game. And he may be resentful of all that fan fuss. Uga has a custom-built air-conditioned dog house and sits on ice bags during the games to keep cool in the deep South."

Amy rattled on about her time at camp. How she liked the instructor Tillman for his endless encouragements. And how she disliked Ms. Walker – "Be sure to address me as Ms." She relished endless star name dropping. Ms. needed to be certain that all the students knew that she knew the great pro players from the past and their expert skills – Steffi Graf's baseline power – Chris Evert's two-hand backhand stroke – Billie Jean King's celebrated defeat over Bobby Riggs. Amy said, "We had to watch that video over n over. But ya gotta admit, it was a winner for us girls forever. I wonder if Coach Simmons at Regional would let me challenge his guys in a public match. Right! I did learn that two-handed backhand from the Chris Evert video. The guys could have reason to worry about me."

"Don't let that home rescue story become me for the year," said Tracy. "It will be a huge year for decisions. For all of us. I'm sure the best kids have already made their college applications and plans. But Amy, I haven't even told you this one. Down in Concord I met with an Air Force Recruiter! He was great to me, very encouraging."

"What! How'd you even get down there? Like me, of

course you have your license, but your dad – he doesn't let you drive his pickup much, right? Certainly not that kind of a trip."

"From my part time job up at the Slater farm, through Jocelyn I've told you all about. Logan Slater's friend Kristen Stanton, she drove us. And of course she was the reason why we were coming back from Vermont that day. From leaving her at her school, the college in Middlebury. Amy, I wish you could see that campus, just like a dream you'd have the way one should be."

Each time one of the friends would tell a catch-up story, she would peel away a small strip of bark from the side of oak stump and toss it out on to the lawn. Amy laughed and said, "My Dad says we'll soon leave these stumps totally bare. Then he says that's a good thing because maybe they'll die. And he won't have to pay for having them removed, you know dug up. Huge roots way under the lawn and a major project. Dad's just tryin to get me goin'. He knows how much I love these stumps. And of course why he kept them. Amy shifted to catch Tracy's eyes, "So -oo, like what about the AF guy, the interview. Tell me everything."

"Well, the recruiter showed us a great video featuring all the speciality possibilities. Way more than I had imagined. Over a hundred. Like for instance Logistics and Mechanics and Flight Training if you are the best of the best. Oh and Intelligence, for the super smart ones. Can you believe it – the one I latched on to was – Rescue Support. How timely is that!" A car passed and they both looked up to wave to Dan Perkins on his way to town for his coffee and donut and his *Manchester Union*. Never missed a morning.

As Tracy was about to tell more of her story, a black

Chevy pickup slowed. The driver carefully eased the truck and right to the curb. A man leaned across the seat and with the passenger window down, he said loud enough to be sure the girls heard him, "Well hey-there girlie-Rousseau. Prob'ly remember me. Right? You and that hot-shot friend of yours. There at the ice cream shop."

The girls remained glued to the stumps – no words, just looking completely dumbfounded. Willie Martin was not sure that his target heard the message fully, so he slid back over in the seat, got out and came around to the sidewalk. He leaned against the telephone pole all casual and unthreatening. No strange camo outfit. Jeans and a plain black sweatshirt but same unlaced boots. He pointed directly to Tracy. "Not gonna bother you at all. I see your hands. No phone I'm guessing. No 911 for me to deal with this time." He stood away from the pole and pointed directly at Tracy. With his same smirk, he said, "Just let your old man Rodney know that I'm still around and ain't forgotten him and that girlfriend of his. Like an elephant, you know – got a real long memory" He stepped down to the road, strode back to the truck and pulled away from the curb. As at the last encounter, no peeling out to invite attention.

Through the afternoon, clouds had thickened and a rain storm was gathering its power along the hills. There were still many oak trees on the property and when the wind stirred itself, it found the tree branches ready for the full-storm dance. As Tracy pulled her bike away from the side of the garage, she waved to Amy on the porch and yelled, "Tell your Dad, oh, oh, more leaves in the morning!" Tracy had spent the rest of the afternoon with Amy worrying over the strange threat from Willie. Her friend had finally convinced her that this time she certainly should tell her father. Tracy resolved to do it after supper at home.

By the time she had reached the house, light rain was falling. She parked her bike in the garage and carefully wiped it down while she rehearsed her story in her mind once more. She feared Dad would maybe just downright explode and rush out to – to what? She hoped that Carol now so much in his life would keep things under control. It pleased her to see the real changes in her dad. She could smell the supper cooking. She put on her calm, there's-no-problem face and opened the garage door to the kitchen. "Hey Carol, I smell something great. I got here just before the storm. It's rolling in."

Carol was over daily now, and both Dad and Tracy enjoyed her cooking. Over the expertly prepared pork chops, mashed potato with hot gravy and green beans, her dad said to Tracy, "You're mighty quiet tonight. I think you told me you'd be seeing friend Amy today. Back from camp, she must have had stories to tell."

"And you and your story about the fire and the medal award, bigger news than hers, I imagine." Carol put her hand up gently when Rodney reached for more salt. She went on, "Tracy, I am still feeling so good for you in all that amazing rescue and the ceremony. That station chief at the award, he just said it all for you and Logan. Great small-town heroics. The lady you and Logan rescued was clearly overcome with appreciation. You surely did help save her life."

"Thank you Carol. It meant a lot to have you there with Dad. Truth is I do have a big something to say after we finish eating. But something very different – and for all three of us. Right after that great blueberry pie I've been eyeing on the counter"

Their living room was simple enough, but it was already showing signs of Carol's touches. Colorful mauve drapes bracketing lacy white curtains, matching throw pillows for the couch and gentle hints about new carpeting one of these days. Rodney said his favorite line whenever that nudge came up. "I might be getting fat, but I'm still sassy." He was clearly in a time of contentment Tracy had never really known. It made for new comfort all around. Settled in her chair by the window, Tracy stalled her uneasy moment by watching the rain drops slide down the window glass. Carol spoke up, "Uh Tracy, you did say you had a something to tell us. Those rain drops will not say a word." Carol had carefully evolved from Dad's Girlfriend to also a mother-like role with Tracy.

Tracy leaned forward and said, "Well Dad, can you believe this – that creepy guy was at it again. Black Chevy pickup and all. Amy and me were just sitting on our favorite stumps, you know out front of her house up by the road. He pulls right to the curb, leans in the cab to us and puts down the window. Then just to be sure I heard it all, he gets out and comes around. Nothing more to call it, he made a real threat to you. To you – and to Carol." Tracy repeated Willie's warning word-for-word.

Rodney leaped to his feet and headed to the kitchen phone. "That's it! I'm calling Chief Denton right now. Gotta be something about – that the chief can do – damn well menacing – that's what it is!"

Carol moved in behind him and put out her hand. "Rodney, hold off. There'll only be the deputy on duty now for the evening. You and I should go right to his office in the morning and tell the chief all of it – from the beginning. This is the second time for us. That brazen show of his pistol at the game. Then again him at the diner makin' sure we saw him. Then remember that he threatened me in town down by LaValle's. Another one of his favorite See-me encounters."

Rodney grasped the edge of a chair to steady himself. More resigned than accepting, he managed to say, "You're probably right. I suppose that's the best way. Face-to-face, we can make our points. Tell Chief the whole story." They both sat back on the couch staring straight ahead, shocked by this latest episode.

Tracy stood and moved to a chair closer to them. Still standing, she let out a "Whoa! You never told me any of this, but be sure, we women do share. Carol even showed me the gun she carries and how you defended her at the park. Scared him off real good. I know that Willie Martin from town. Kids know things." She paused and checked to see if Carol revealed that she was unhappy with this unexpected revelation. A smile and a nod brought an okay. She sat and went on, "Dad, this is actually my second time with that same guy."

"What! That slug! I need to –"

Carol held him back tightly by the arm. "Let her tell it, Rodney. Maybe you'll want her to go with us to the chief tomorrow."

"We're learning something about us, Dad. You didn't tell me any of this and like father, like daughter, I didn't tell you either. We're usually feeling 'the less upset, the better' I guess." She sat and began the story about Willie Martin at the ice cream stand. "The day that Kristen took me to Concord to see the Air Force Recruiter, on the way home we stopped at I-Scream across from Owens Field. Kristen and I were sitting at one of the outdoor tables enjoying our treat. This guy comes up and just invites himself right in to our table! We were shocked! He was way overdressed for a hot summer evening – camo jacket and hat, big ol boots untied. Just a weird lookin' guy. He said you and him had what he called 'a little misunderstanding.' That's what he called it, those very words. But it was his like, you know, his insulting tone that was clear, way beyond the words. Smart-guy manner. 'aggressive and arrogant' are the words Kristen used later."

Carol had to hold Rodney's arm firmly to keep him from heading for the phone again. She was maintaining the calm like a wife and a mother. She said, "Go ahead Tracy, finish the story."

"So before the guy could say another word, Kristen pulled the cell phone from her purse. She stared him right in the eyes and said, 'Watch it fella – I'm one move from dialing 911.'" He backed off in a real hurry. But as he moved away, he turned and said in a, you know, real threatening way – 'Tell your dad that more days are comin' and for that girlfriend too.' And this too was weird, he already knew my name and called me by it. That really shocked us to start with."

Rodney could not be held back. He jumped to his feet and strode across the room. By the opening to the kitchen, he stopped and whirled back. He said in a voice trembling with anger, "We'll damn sure have a case to tell to the chief. I won't be sleepin' too good tonight." He went on to the kitchen and opened the cabinet door above the sink.

Carol knew what was coming next. She moved quickly behind him and said, "You've been doing so great with that. To drink now would be to surrender to that ugly man. To be saying 'you got me after all.' "

Rodney slumped down into a chair and put his head down into his hands. Carol came up behind him and gently rubbed his shoulders. She leaned forward and said softly, "We're the ones in control here. This will all come out right,"

From her chair in the living room, Tracy saw this whole thing play out. She fastened on one thought – *Willie Martin you have brought my dad a real gift in ways you'll never know.*

~ ~ ~

Rodney liked that his mowing and plowing jobs were flexible, and he could move his times around readily for this interview. Carol's Impala was the choice when more than a pickup's room was needed. She parked in Visitors and they climbed the steps to the police department wing. The town board had wisely put the fire department in the same building, engines on the lower level. They were greeted by the office deputy. Rodney and Carol and yes, Tracy as well as so much a part of these incidents. She led them to the door, frosted window top panel stenciled modestly, Chief Walter Denton. Remaining behind his desk, the chief stood to his full height and said, "Excellent, right at ten as we agreed. We keep a tight schedule as we can here." He gestured to the padded chairs in front of his desk.

Tracy could feel her heart thumping away. She tried to notice everything so she could tell Amy. But sorry, no tv-style suspects along chairs in the wait area. Chief's office was pretty expected stuff. Computer, printer and fax machine on a side desk. His phone with its array of buttons next to a photo of him and a German shepherd dog. She wished she dared ask him about the dog. And no, not even a half empty box of donuts like the standard myth. Rodney and Carol were ready to speak directly, but Tracy had prepared notes. She held on to them like a vital theater prop.

The chief listened to the accounts of Willie's threats with full professional attention. He asked incisive questions and took notes. Actually Carol kept her calm better than Rodney was able to. She eased him down with gentle touches to his arm when his face grew red, and he seemed ready to pound the desk in anger. He resisted, knowing that definitely would not help his case.

When Tracy spoke, her voice quivered slightly – as in a book report in front of the class. But the more she moved into the details of incidents with Willie, the stronger she became. She told how Kristen pulled out her phone and threatened to call 911. How that threat scared him off. She felt her notes helped with actual quotes.

But then the chief said firmly, "Your friend really should have dialed the 911. Officer Ainsworth would have come right away. With your description of Willie Martin and of his truck, we would have pulled him over. Truth is we know him pretty well. Small town and all. He's been on the very edge of trouble for a long time." Tracy was sorry for the professional reprimand, but she was relieved to hear that he was known to the police.

Tracy was determined to tell every situation. She said, "Sir, there was still another time. My friend from school

Moving On

Amy Lowry and I were sitting on our favorite stumps in front of her house on Emmons Street. We were like just watching the day go by and catching up. And – "

The chief nodded and said, "I know that neighborhood well, a pleasant one." He stayed to the business at hand though he certainly knew about Tracy's bravery award. "Please go on."

Tracy brushed that obstinate strand of hair back and continued, "So Amy was just, you know, telling me about her tennis camp. Then a black pickup pulled right to the curb near us. I knew for sure that truck and that driver. It was Willie Martin." She told how they were both scared and yet somehow not so much. His manner seemed to them all bluster. Like the school bullies. She checked her notes to make certain of what he had said. "He pointed his finger at me and said, 'Just let your ol man Rodney know that I'm still around and ain't forgotten him and that girlfriend of his. Like an elephant, you know – got a real long memory.' "

The chief took more notes, then looked up with a slight smile and said, "H'mm, like an elephant."

Rodney spoke last believing that his account would be the vital information revealing that Willie threatened with a gun. He told of the incident at the Owens Park Little League game. How the guy was really bothering Carol. Then that smug showing of the butt of his gun tucked into his belt. Chief Denton leaned right forward on that revelation. He said, "Serious information like that is extremely crucial. We will immediately review his records. He'd definitely need a concealed-carry permit. New Hampshire, all states actually, have very specific legal regulations for it. However, no one made any charges for this incident. You, Rodney, as you are telling it, did not assault him really. Actually it was battery, physical handling as you know. He could have made a charge and a possible civil suit. But! Had he pulled his pistol out – then it would have been a very different matter altogether, for certain."

Carol spoke up, "Knowing that guy, he'd claim self-defense and all that complicated – Wouldn't he?"

~ ~ ~

"Let's not speculate on that possible very bad scene. Rest assured, I will have a nice conversation with Willie Martin. Not here in my office. No, I like to go to the place of residence. It gives me a chance to have a good look about. Nothing comfortable like we've had here today." The chief stood and the three thanked him and left.

Back in Carol's car, Rodney spoke up first, "We are mighty fortunate to have Chief Denton. His family goes back years in the town. If it wasn't for that, an ex-Marine, he'd could have moved up to – well, maybe even FBI."

Carol nodded and said, "Tall and commanding like that, Willie will be quaking in his boots. Those very scruffy boots. They're one of his comfortable trademarks I guess."

From the back seat, Tracy added, "That's right. Yes, those boots he always keeps untied. I don't get that. What are they untied for – a quick bare-foot getaway?"

As she reached down to start the car, Rodney put his hand out for her to pause. He said, "Good thing we had agreed not to say anything about the gun you bought after that scene at the park. I imagine the chief would have had a few words for you as in 'Don't do anything stupid!' At least you were smart to leave it home today. He'll check records on us both of course."

Moving On

Carol refused to bite. They had hashed that issue over and over. Instead, she smartly jumped to a new topic. She said over her shoulder, "Well, Tracy, too bad Chief Denton doesn't have a son at the high school. He'd be tall n handsome for certain."

Her first impulse was to answer, "Like I'd really have any chance." She passed over that weak response with, "Well maybe I could've given that project a nice run, especially with Senior Prom coming in the spring." That was the new Tracy speaking.

14

Jocelyn greeted Tracy at the door. "Well now, the brave one is back with me. Tracy, that ceremony in Vermont was so impressive and so well deserved. For both you and Logan. Let's sit in the kitchen, and you can tell me more. Kurt and I talked about the award over and over on the drive back."

Tracy was having another one of those good days, "Half the reason why that day was so great – beyond the medal and the words – was having people I care about there. Of course Logan, you and Kurt, Kristen and my Dad and Carol. That's my whole summer life!"

"You know that is quite the cast of characters and you're right, we've all had some part in your summer's experience. You'll have lots of essay material for certain." She smiled and put her hand on Tracy's shoulder. She added, "Probably leave out that thing with Hitler and the dart board though. Very complicated to explain." They both laughed, and it gave Tracy reassurance to know that incident had kept an okay level of their shared past.

In the kitchen they sat at the table, the special comfort zone. Jocelyn said, "We do have a full day of chores, but they can wait."

"Well, school does begin next week, and I'm very ready

for my final year. – But I'm sad too. This will be the end of my daily times with you. Come summer after my graduation, who knows – My dad says he will take me down before Thanksgiving to the community college in St Johnsbury. That's over in Vermont like Kristen's college. Carol convinced her dad that if I want the Air Force, the more education I can show, the stronger are my chances. She actually repeated what the recruiter said almost word for word. And she wasn't even there."

"At the rescue ceremony, we were very pleased to meet your dad and Carol. It should have happened long before. Back when you came to us for the after-school job, you remember I called Rodney. I asked him if he wanted to meet to be assured everything was, you know, all good for you and for us." She slid away the coffee cup she'd been nursing. "Gone totally cold now. Actually, Rodney said he was okay with your job with us. Then he added a strange remark I have never told you. He said, "Well, sometimes Tracy does just what she damn well pleases to do. Like her mother.' I certainly had no response for that remark."

Tracy showed no surprise at all. She said, "There were lots of times that stuff like that came out between us, my mother and me. Now I realize it was more about her, than about me. Dad was so hurt by her sudden up-and-out. I'm sure that was why he was drinking like that." She reached across to touch Jocelyn's hand – a gesture completely unnatural for the old Tracy. She went on, "Yes, that mother did just plain disappear. But in an amazing way, I have found not one but two to take her place. Carol is steady and calm and supports me in so many ways. And the real thing, she has changed Dad, not just the drinking but his whole life, it seems like – contented now like never in the past." She stood and said, "Jocelyn, you are my other mother. This year with you has changed my life."

Tracy's job for the morning was one more round of cleaning in the basement collection. It had been a full week and the dust somehow always seemed to find its favored spots. The spider webs too sneaked daily along the shelf racks if you didn't whisk them away. Later for that. Tracy pulled out the vacuum. That job required great carefulness around the treasures. When she finished with the vac needs, she sat near a little display Harry had placed beneath a poster he had printed in big block letters. It read: <u>New Hampshire Claims The Oval Office.</u> The first time Tracy had scanned over the records below the poster, she was downright smug that she knew there could be only one president in history who could make that claim – Franklin Pierce.

She read on some of the history he had preserved beside a photo copy of the president. A handsome man, she noted. Reading on, she found that New Hampshire's only president had served the country from 1833 to 1837, a single term. It pleased her to discover that he was born in a log cabin. Even from fifth grade, the log cabin part of President Lincoln's life was special to all the kids, how he read by candlelight and knew his Bible with an amazing memory that helped him all his life. She discovered more parallels with President Lincoln: they both were lawyers and that during Pierce's time also the huge, troubling slavery issue dominated the country, leading up to that awful Civil War.

One more thing caught her eye. That Harry Kaiser was

such a meticulous one for detail. He had included a photo copy of the famous writer Nathaniel Hawthorne with the side comment, "A lifetime friend of Franklin Pierce. Both graduated Bowdoin College in Maine." Tracy thought back again to Junior English with Mr. Billings. They had read Hawthorne's *The Scarlet Letter*. Some kids liked it. Some hated it. Tracy and Amy both liked it. Amy got a 92 on the test and Tracy an 83, one of her better grades.

Although she had promised herself to stay away from the gun display, she rediscovered that self-promises often lose in struggles with temptation.

It pleased her again that Jocelyn now found it maybe even funny – that catching her pointing the Luger at the Hitler dart board. Her eyes wandered over to a revolver Harry had labeled with a touch of his humor: "This six-shooter is just like the one used by Hop-along Cassidy, my favorite film cowboy." Then in smaller print he had typed: "I liked him over Roy Rogers because he didn't kiss the women he saved. I thought Gabby Hayes was a great funny-guy character too." Next to the photo of his kid-days hero was a lunch box with a Hop-along picture on it. She said aloud, "Wow! Even had that fun lunch-box thing in the old days."

Tracy marveled again at what a range of topics Harry found so fascinating that he seemed determined to save them in his collections. Each item pushed her into popular or serious history while revealing so much about the collector himself. Along with the stories Kurt and Logan told of their personal time with Harry, it made her feel as if she too had known him, as even a nice grandpa.

Beside the Hop-along Cassidy display, was a long rifle

and a photo of Annie Oakley, someone from time past Tracy knew nothing about. The page with the photo told her that Annie Oakley was at an early age an expert with a rifle and went on to be a star in the Buffalo Wild West Show and became so famous, she even showed her skills to presidents and to Queen Victoria on her Golden Jubilee.

Tracy knew she needed to get on with her work, but discovering that this woman was a famous marksman impressed her. It made her puzzle again why guns brought on her these mixed feelings – the troubling ones and the strange attraction. Now that she knew that Carol even carried one – she'd need to hear more from Carol on that decision for certain. As she turned away, she noticed that a spider web was making its way under the shelf section. She hoped not to discover its owner. It snapped her back to reality.

Upstairs over a lunch of chicken salad and iced tea, Jocelyn continued her role as mentor, but remained careful about not pushing too much. She knew that teens sometimes take restriction efforts by, of course, doing just the opposite. She remembered Ben Franklin on that subject – *the lad seeks independence while the father seeks control.* She understood full well that the basement does not need these frequent cleanings. She has focused on its real purpose – providing a "classroom of life" for Tracy to discover on her own. As she set the salad plates down, Jocelyn said, "Look at us, eating like we were prepping for a movie role, no hamburgers and French fries for us. So then Tracy, how much dust and spider webbing did you wipe away down there this morning?"

"Actually some of both, but it's amazing how the dust

and webs lead me right to distractions and learning neat stuff." She did her familiar eye-roll with brows right up for the fun doubts. "Probably not part of any plan by someone. Right?" Mentor, friend and mother role had moved the two to read each other well.

Jocelyn squeezed the lemon into her tea and swirled the ice cubes, a favorite thinking stall. Finally she said, "Well, it surely worked for Logan and Harry. Kurt has told me great stories of how Logan would get so – you know, totally immersed in some of the displays. He even startled Harry with his being way too "there" in the scenes. Once he seemed to virtually go over the Niagara Falls after hearing about the true story of the young boy who survived it."

"Nothing that real for me, but it's like watching great tv documentaries – you know *National Geographic* or *Animal Planet* only I get to choose and move on whenever I want to. She exchanged an aw-shucks- you-got-me-look and said, "Naturally I mean move on to another dust clump. Probably I should vacuum next week. Anyway today I finished with a history lesson about Annie Oakley. She was so amazingly skilled with a rifle. She was famous for The Buffalo Bill shows and even in Europe."

Jocelyn used the tea ice again for a delayed answer. She said, "I am curious though, Tracy, is it just a coincidence – or could it may be a pattern. You are surely attracted to guns – the German luger, the Hitler target and now Annie Oakley.

Her Dad or Carol had never told Tracy that the Willie Martin threats could not be shared with someone she trusts. And certainly her friend Amy already was in a part of it. "Well, we may need refills on this one. But I do want to tell you. You met Carol and my dad at the awards. Truth is we all have had some weird threats by an odd guy Willie Martin in town. Carol even carries a pistol in her purse now, legal of course. Dad hates guns but that Willie, he has this thing about getting even for a fight they had at Owens Park. That's how he met Carol, the real good thing that has come out of it. But that guy, he has a gun and showed it in the fight and — "

"Hold on right there, Tracy. Has your dad gone to the police, to Chief Denton?"

"All three of us met with him. Willie got Carol again and me and Kristen and me and my friend Amy once too. Just nasty threatening, no direct — . The chief was great, and he's going to follow up with what he called 'a home interview' of Willie Martin."

Jocelyn reached across the table for Tracy's hand. She said, "And you can always come to me. You need to know that. I am not going to tell Kurt about this right now anyway. He's a man of action, and he might try to get involved. Seems like there's no need for more complications. Going to the police like you did was a smart move."

~ ~ ~

By the Pet Stuff store, the chief eased the cruiser to the curb in the perfect open spot, right behind Willie Martin's Chevy pickup. He sat behind the wheel for a few moments considering his purpose and life in small towns. He knew it did not at all mirror the extensive police challenges in cities, but when he responded to domestic violence calls or break-ins, unlike the city, he knew these people sometimes very personally — even friends, neighbors and school buddies.

"Aw c'mon now, Chief, you know me" was an ever-present troublesome plea in his role. The state police and the county were there for his support when needed.

He got out and inspected the taillights on the truck and nodded approval. Walking up the stairs to Willie's apartment, he noted them as clean and safe. With only two apartments in the building, it was simple to find Willie's. Down the hall would be Mrs. Canister's double and knowing her, that was why the stairs were clean and the hallway too. There were no black plastic garbage bags awaiting a trip to the dumpster in back. In Willie's favor, if he was granted rent by Mrs. Canister, he must have passed her careful inspection.

Chief liked to catch these intensive chats with the "person of interest" just as they lived day-to-day. No heads-up call. He knocked firmly and knew that Willie had already checked him out through the door eye-hole. The door opened immediately. Hat under his arm, full equipment belt with pistol in polished holster, the sharp pressed uniform, the six-foot three, it was all definitely imposing. Willie stood there looking downright surprised and very uncomfortable. Chief said, "Chief Denton, Mr. Martin, I am sure you know me from town. Near five, so I expected you'd be home from your job."

~ ~ ~

Willie knew he needed to give full attention, but he half tried a quick glance back around at his rumpled rooms. Trying to sound both casual but intruded upon, he managed an unconvincing, "Chief – whatever – you know – what ever brings you here to visit me – may I ask? Oh that damn truck again? Fixed that taillight a week ago. I told Officer

Ainsworth I would – and I did."

The chief invited himself in with several steps closer. Wille back peddled trying to keep a space between himself and serious authority. No untied boots, just white socks, a wrinkled tee shirt and khakis. The chief said, "No, no, Mr. Martin, no truck problems. I looked at your taillight before I came up. I check all the reports, even the minor ones." He was face-to-face now. "However, we may have a major problem here. Three residents in town have come to me with a detailed account of a series of what seem to be – actual serious threats. This may take some time. Can we sit?"

Willie was on the edge of threatened himself. He retreated to his table which doubled as his eating spot, his newspaper time and his catch-all. He swept up the take-out food cartons and tossed them into the trash basket. He gestured to the only other chair he had. Never the one facing the door. He'd seen enough John Wayne movies to know to always face the door. Now across from each other, it looked like a job interview. The chief rested his hat on the table and sat still at military attention. He said, "So Mr. Martin, I am sure you know this is about Rodney Rousseau, his friend Carol Girard and especially about a minor, his daughter Tracy."

Willie hoped the sweat easing around his hairline would not be as obvious as he suspected it was. This was way worse than his boss pulling him in for being late twice in one week. Way worse than Principal LeBeau standing and peering down at him for fighting in the hall in those unpleasant days. Trying to be very cool and confident, he said, "Ah that Rousseau, me and him had just a little scuffle

159

at Owens Park. You know over a woman who thought I was being, you know, comin' on too hard to her. Rousseau, he was a big baseball star at the school in his time there. He just wanted to play hero. Didn't mean no – didn't expect her to get all testy like. Tryin to be friendly is all." Willie struggled to make eye contact. His mother always knew when he was lying. She used to say, "Those eyeballs seem to like that floor too much, Willie."

The chief tapped his fingers on the table and said, "Well even if I accept that version, both Mr. Rousseau and Ms. Girard made it very clear that you showed the butt of a pistol in your belt. In a definitely threatening manner."

"You know Rousseau from his baseball days, right, chief? He's a real big guy, way bigger than me. Well, I guess I must have showed the pistol, but I swear, I never pulled it out. And! Next thing I know, he whacked me a beaut up right against the fence!"

"And you did what then?"

"I beat it outta there. That self-defense stuff is a real tough one these days. Didn't need that in my life. I imagine you checked and found I've got all the permits in order for my gun. But I know enough not to threaten direct with it."

"Yes, you certainly did the smart thing at the time." The chief pulled a small notebook from his pocket. He said, "The daughter assured me that you threatened her again at the ice cream shop. You apparently invited yourself to sit across from her and her friend at an outside table. Then threatened that you knew who she was and to pass on to her father and Ms. Girard a message of – what was that really – a message of planned revenge? Come on now, Mr. Martin, a teenager having a pleasant day and you put that on her."

"Ah, just havin' some fun I guess. My life is pretty dull so when things come up – "

"Odd bit of fun. And then still another incident with the daughter and her friend – he checked his notes – Amy Lowry – sitting outside on Emmons Street and you pulled over to the curb and made the same threats. I'm using the word threat here in all these accusations. Mr. Martin, there is nothing I can legally charge you with – at this time. But keep smart. Stay fully away from these people. I know you go to the gun range and Bud Foster, Sarge, there has only good to say about you. Yes, be certain that I checked that too. Make that your only gun use. I am sure you understand me here. Do I have that correct?"

What could Willie say. He knew it was all true. He nodded and said a weak, "Yes, sir, you do" and tried to look away.

The chief stood and said to close. "Seems you have a good place here and convenient parking." He passed on noting that it could use a thorough cleaning up. "We're a small town and generally law-abiding. We all like to keep it peaceful. Be relieved that I don't report this to the building owner. Mrs. Canister is known for her careful ways. You surely know that." Chief reached for his hat and turned for the door.

Willie collapsed back into his chair. His head buzzed with – what next – be smart like the chief warned – or be real careful with that Rousseau. He still needed to get that finally out of his craw.

~ ~ ~

Kurt had Mondays off from Joe's in exchange for working Saturdays to catch the customers who used that day for major errands. It would not be long before snow tires would be their lively business again. "Dummies waiting for the first flakes" was a joke he and Joe enjoyed. Kurt had been at Joe's much longer than he ever intended. He still thought of the job as temporary. He promised himself to not be locked in. Tracy was finishing her summer days coming to help Jocelyn. With school next week, she'd be down mainly to Saturdays.

Kurt met Tracy in the kitchen and said, "The Boss, she is letting me have your help for the morning. We're old-fashioned New Hampshire farmers today." Out on the back patio as they passed the glads, he said, "With your real job at school for your – whoa , can it be – your senior year – you will miss a great outdoor treat with me. Harry taught me how to carefully dig these flower bulbs, called corms, and put them to sleep in the cellar room for the winter. For their new life in the spring. Perfect time is after the first frost but before serious freeze. He was such a good man with always his sense of humor mixed with his useful advice. He'd say, 'The bulbs will hibernate along with the bears.' Maybe we will plan that for a Saturday. Course Mother Nature is very choosy about her timing."

Tracy loved hearing about Mr. Kaiser. She said, "Well, you can imagine how I am actually getting to feel he's a friend through the Collection. I'm sure you know that each special item is fascinating in itself, but it always, you know, reveals like something about him."

They walked from the patio to the vegetable garden as it stretched toward the field. Kurt said, "I guess Jocelyn has told you that Harry and Lillian, she was in on all the outdoor projects, they used to have an extensive cornfield beyond these veggie sections, and she had a home stand by the road. But they dropped that phase of their lives – well especially as he got older and into his years of retirement. Corn is a commanding and difficult project – unless of course you're massive Kellogg farms in the Midwest. Deer n the crows are eager corn chasers." The cornfield had now gone to grass, but Kurt and Logan would never forget its meaning for them – yes, like thieves, sneaking along through it in the night and changing their lives forever.

Tracy spoke up, "Jocelyn said Mrs. Kaiser loved a vegetable stand out front. Kept her teacher urges alive with customers when she was off for summers."

"Well, we won't have a stand but that's our project. This morning we're going to find the last of the cukes and the summer squash and check on the pumpkins with you-know-what coming. Not like we're going to going to have families with kids chasing about seeking the perfect prize for carving. That's a great scene though. We only have a few for Jocelyn to bring down to her church group. I'm not the farmer that Harry was of course, and I don't have the time. But who knows, maybe we'll retire up here someday. Still have his snowmobiles for the winter fun."

Tracy responded to that idea, "Sounds like a plan. I'll come and visit you in my Air Force uniform." She even avoided the standard teen caveat about herself, the "Sure – right?"

On their knees, Tracy and Kurt found scattered long, green cucumbers and curved yellow squash to toss into the basket. They checked the pumpkins and found that sufficient rain and sun in August had fattened them up. Tracy wandered the patch and stopped at an especially plump one. She kneeled over it and felt the warm morning rays on her back. She said, "Please Kurt, you gotta save this one out for me. Maybe Jocelyn and I will carve some smiley faces. My dad and I used to do that back in my trick-or-treat days, but I guess it slipped away. You know, me getting like too old for it."

She saw that Kurt's eyes showed some regret. Maybe for his lost-dad days. She hastened to add, "Oh we still answer the door with the candy. Several good kids on our street, but we don't like it when a few mothers pull up a van full from across town. New eight o'clock curfew for that is great. But anyway our pumpkin is plastic." She moved the leaves aside and patted her fat selected prize, then stood and placed her hands on her hips. She feigned an in-charge look. "Just you be sure, dibs is a big deal you know."

Kurt gestured to a hole in the edge of the garden and said, "See that hole? It's an old burrow nest for pesky woodchucks. Naturally, they raided the veggies and sometimes cleared a big number of em. Just enough bites to destroy any use. Like all famers, Harry was a great shot and wanted to blast em with his shotgun. Lillian wouldn't let him, so he went to a second plan, used commonly by farmers. You back the tractor or a truck up to the site, attach a long hose to the exhaust pipe and insert it into the burrow. I guess you are getting the idea now. Start er up and the exhaust gasses those pests right to critter eternity."

Tracy put her hand to her mouth and cringed, "Oh my God, that is not a scene I'd care to see! Well, I suppose it may be better than being shot and maybe hit in the leg and running off to die. That's probably what Mrs. K objected to, right?"

"Well actually, that fine woman even opposed the deer hunting, but she had no support from Harry on that one." Kurt had a flash thought to add about the woodchucks – Just like the gas chamber for murderers, but he passed on that dark comparison. However, he could not resist and said, "But no governor's last hour pardon for them."

As the two of them moved to the house with the basket, now overflowing with the vegetables, Tracy stumbled and half fell into a bush beside the patio. She recovered the fall easily, but suddenly the air was full of angry wasps buzzing around her head. Kurt steadied her and said, "Don't swat at em, just back away. They're real stirred up and mad of course. But good old Harry told me, 'Find the nest later and spray at night when they're all home with their queen.' " They both inched away from of the attack zone and reached the patio without ever spilling the basket.

Pointing to the bench, Kurt said, "Let's sit for awhile. That could have been really painful if you'd of got stung. More country lore – wasps do not have stingers like honey bees so there is nothing to try to remove. But it could really hurt for a while. Supposed to put ice on it for swelling and some lotion for the itch that will come, maybe calamine." He looked back over his shoulder to see if she had seen them through the sliding screen. He said, "Jocclyn would know from her apple orchard days as a kid. She was a farmer too you know. Ladders in the orchard, tractors, canning the tomatocs, the whole thing ."

Tracy had seen the *Apple Blossoms* painting in charcoal many times and had heard the stories of James Kaiser, the known artist. Never thought of its secret kept by Kurt and Logan only. She said, "You can be sure my dad has had his times with wasps and bees. When he mows and trims all through the summer. He calls the wasps yellow jackets. Well sometimes stronger words. Same guys as wasps right?"

"I haven't heard that name since kid days, but I'm sure they are. Probably from the color. Like all those great snake rhymes." He wiped his forehead with a colorful handkerchief. "So here we are, just like two farmers. We should have hoes to lean on as we admire our crops." Then more seriously, "I don't get much time with you. Mostly my sense of things about you Tracy is from Jocelyn." Kurt was good at friendly conversation as part of his job. Usually though that chatter was about what tires are the best and naturally trucks and the weather. He turned to her and said, "So you are serious about this Air Force thing? I got those details via Kristen on to Jocelyn."

Tracy had agreed to not tell the threat part of that trip to the recruiter. That weird thing with Willie Martin at the ice cream shop. Instead, she centered on Kristen. "Kristen was so great with me that day and before in the summer. You know that she and Logan took me to the Franconia Notch to ride the Tramway. Never will forget that day!" She paused to consider how far to go and decided to charge ahead. "Uh, do you think Logan and Kristen are, you know – steadies in a serious way? Maybe even to be married someday. They seem to be a perfect couple. They even correct each other's remarks, like you know, old married types."

Kurt smiled as a church pastor would, all knowing, but not saying. "Well the truth is, I'm the last one to predict the future. Had my troubles doing that some time back.

Anyway, you kids just live for the moment, right?"

Tracy finished the day helping Jocelyn clean the prized veggies. Late afternoon, Kurt said he would drive her home. In the truck, they were both quiet, having talked themselves out during the morning. But she still wished she had dared to bring up one more topic. She knew it would probably be way too personal and awkward. Truth is she had never even asked the question to Jocelyn for the same reasons. What she wanted to come right out with was, "Gee, Kurt, I keep wondering about, you know, about you and Jocelyn – well like uh, maybe having a baby. Starting a family." Possibly the answer would come by itself. She settled on that pleasant thought.

As they approached the driveway to her house, Tracy said, "Oh don't try to drive in. Not much room with Carol's car there. Nice Impala, isn't it? And I really enjoyed the day with you." She laughed. "Yes, being an old-fashioned New Hampshire farmer." She waved to him as Kurt pulled away. Reaching her front steps, she heard another car, exhaust rumbling along the street. No! Not a car. A black Chevy pickup. That one! Willie Martin pulled off along the edge of the lawn, parked and hopped out. Shocked – she froze to the spot on the stoop and grabbed for the steps rail.

~ ~ ~

"Hey!" he yelled. "Hey – really – no harm meant at all. Need just to talk to you – and really mostly to your father."

Tracy recovered her sense of balance and stood by the door with her hand on the doorknob as protection. She faced the intruder directly and held her ground. "Are you crazy! We know that Chief Denton warned you about this kind of thing. This threatening. My dad will be out in one second if I open this door. Then you'll be done!"

"No, no go ahead open up. See if he will come out to talk."

Tracy half turned and opened the door slowly all the while watching for any sudden moves. Dad was sitting in the den watching tv. She could see Carol beyond in the kitchen. Tracy tried to be casual, not wanting to alarm her father. She said loudly enough to be heard through the door, "Dad, could you come out here please. I need some help. Really. Right now."

In a flash, Rodney was out to the steps. Seeing this stunning sight, he yelled, "What ta hell! You! What do ya think you're doing now – right on my property!"

With Rodney on the steps landing already taller and far more rugged, Willie on ground level looked weak and vulnerable. He struggled to show his determination. Not high-tail it as was his common response.

"Please there Rodney, I'm sure you know by now that the chief visited me. He made it very clear that I need to, you know, move on past these – well – uh – yes – he called them a series of threats. Guess you know this too. Nobody messes with the chief."

Carol had heard the commotion and rushed to the door. Amazed at the scene, turning back she said, "I'm getting my phone and my purse." Both Rodney and Tracy knew full well what was in that purse. In seconds she was back at the open door. Phone in one hand. Gun in the other.

Between Rodney's overwhelming size advantage and now a gun pointed right at him – Willie fought his gut instinct to run. Something gave him the maybe foolish courage to hold his place. He put up one hand palm out, not the hands-up position. He pleaded. "No, no gun – needed here at all. Mine is in the truck. And no 911. That's why I came. Want to tell you that I'm done with it. Won't never be near you again. You know like a protection order. I can see that you never really needed one. The phone – sure – but now a woman with a gun!"

Willie wanted to say one more thing, "Everybody in town has heard of your daughter's rescue award over there in Vermont." He pointed to Tracy. "Gotta give ya credit, damn strong stuff. And take my word, I'm out of your lives." He had said his piece. He did not wait for a response. He turned and walked straight to his truck.

The three stood at the door now more stunned than ever. Finally Rodney said, "Can you believe that! The chief must have put the fear of God into that guy."

Tracy turned to Carol and said, "Really, Carol did you know what you were going to do – with that gun!"

Rodney put up his hand in an "Enough" sign. He said, "We need to go in and make some sense out of all this scene. And Carol, please put that thing away!"

They found their usual spots inside around the kitchen table, best for face-to-face. Rodney spoke first, "Truth now, Carol, was that revolver of yours even loaded? I hope you don't carry it around in your purse loaded."

"Come-on Rodney, what good is it not loaded. You may not like guns, but you certainly know what the safety is for. And the times, they are changin'. These days you can never know what may come your way – unwanted ."

Rodney let it go at that. He and Carol had had this discussion many times before. He looked carefully at Tracy and said, "I hope you're okay. Must have scared you like crazy at first. Tell me exactly how he approached you. What did he say?"

Tracy assured her father that she was okay but certainly shocked by the whole thing. She repeated what Willie said and that knowing she was one open door away from help, made it more strange than disturbing.

"But Rodney," Carol asked, "whatever do you make of these pleas and promises he made? All very out of his dealings with us. Is this a guy to trust at his word?"

"It's not anything to bring to the chief yet again. I guess we need to take him at his word. But be always careful. Tracy will be back to school next week. That should be fine for her." He spread his fingers out on the table, then doubled them into a fist. "I doubt he wants to take me on again. Actually, when you think about it, he has never really done anything. But he did make sure we know he has a gun. All threat stuff and lurking around like he thinks he's some kind of an undercover agent or something. Maybe that's his plan. Keeping us constantly uneasy. You know to get even for what was really a typical little – not even a fight really. Pretty pathetic all in all." He stood to show he had no more to say.

Willie kept to the speed limit all the way back to his apartment. He took a long way around though to completely enjoy this new sense of control. To plain swell up with how it all went ... got em good ... now I'll pick my time for some real stuff ... them all relaxed and not expectin' ... nobody will make me look like a fool ever again ... He parked in his usual spot. The Pet Stuff store was usually not all that busy.

Striding with new confidence bounding up his stairs, at

the top he nearly ran into Mrs. Canister. She popped up her hands and said, "Whoa there, Willie. I knocked on your door but no answer. Of course, because here you are. It's just near tea time. Not busy? Walk down with me. We'll have a nice chat like we do. I know you like my chocolate chip cookies with the tea."

She was certainly not his actual aunt, but Willie allowed himself to sail along with the fantasy. It pleased him to have this newly found friend and especially someone to talk to without any complications. Mrs. C, as he called her, had poured the hot tea British style. She made a grand ritual of it. Sugar in the cup first, then a thinly sliced lemon, then the tea and the milk the very last touch. "I'm sure The Queen takes it just like that and maybe even wants to pour her own. A remarkable long and successful reign for her."

All his adult life, Willie drank coffee or Pepsi right out of the can, never tea. But he wanted to be favored, to be this casual friend. A pretty small sacrifice for that role, and he was actually getting to enjoy the tea and always the cookies. Mrs. C. had even promised British style scones but they had not yet appeared.

She reached for a book she had on the lamp table, its red tasseled marker was showing her page. She moved her hand over the book almost lovingly and said, "I'm reading my way through the presidents. Well the ones I like anyway. This time it's Dwight Eisenhower. Now you, Willie, you've driven the interstates. Did you know that it was President Eisenhower who established the impetus for that system? To be certain in time of war, God forbid yet another one, we could transport efficiently from coast to coast. A fine military leader and truly good man." She had opened to a picture of the president and continued, "Dwight is a name you do not hear anymore. She closed the book and looked more directly at her guest, "This reminds me, I have been interested why your parents chose the name Willie. Is it a variation of William to Willie, not Billy?"

Willie was overwhelmingly pleased with her personal interest in him. A rare experience in his life as an adult. He said, "No, actually it's just plain Willie, no William or Billy. My father wanted nothing to do with the naming – or with me much either. That's a different story for another time. Anyway, my mother chose Willie because she liked the country singer Willie Nelson. I have sometimes wondered if that was because she really wanted to be 'on the road again,' Willie Nelson's famous song and lifestyle. That would have been neat for both of us. Her fantasy life, I guess. We all have one. Instead, she stayed home and more or less served my father as women were expected to do then. Big changes in that now."

Mrs. C. replaced the book on her stand carefully and said, "That was most interesting, so here's another question. Do you read? On my shelf there, I have one of the absolute best ever. *John Adams* by that wonderful biographer David McCullough. I could lend it to you for an excellent start to these fascinating presidential lives. Then for New Hampshire, you'd go on to President Franklin Pierce. Maybe you could visit the Pierce home down in Concord."

"Willie tried to show that he had not completely wasted his time at school. He said, "Well, we always got Washington and Lincoln. Seems like every grade from fifth on. But those others, they are a little vague to me. Oh, Teddy

Roosevelt, I do remember him and the Rough Riders." He sipped his tea cradling the cup awkwardly fearful of any drippings. Mrs. C. did not pick him up on it. He settled back in the comfortable chair and with his new confidence, he said, "Your timing today is just perfect for me. Truth is I've had me a little trouble over the past weeks. You are such a good listener, let me start from kid days to give it the full idea. I was, you could say, a little chubby in school. You know how certain bully types are constantly on the lookout for anything they can rub in. Glasses, noses, how you walk, how you dress, that's always a favorite. Something mean on your brother or sister or even your folks."

Mrs. C. shook her head. "I have such sadness for that bullying cycle. It goes back in history of course. Some of the schools in England, terrible cruelty even from the Head Masters." She wanted to change the subject. You said 'provocative' – that is just a fine word. A librarian's life you know is words and people, both the ones on paper and the ones who come to search and have a question for us. I put a quick stop to any meanness in my library. Of course we always checked the stacks where they think they are hidden. Or fool me from behind a book? Not likely. Anyway, go on with your story."

Willie was eager to make this part clear, "Well, the thing that started my hate for this particular guy, this Rodney Rousseau, was a fight we had at Owens Park. a few weeks back." Willie described the complete humiliation he felt especially since the woman was right there cheering on the rescue. The more he told, the angrier he got, red face and at times voice a bit too loud for a nice lady's living room. No pounding on her tea table for certain. He gradually calmed himself and said, "Talk about how things have a way. I guess it was me who brought him and that woman, that Carol Girard, together as, you know, as a couple." He swept his hand across his chest and added smartly, "She don't know it, but she missed out on a way better chance. What's this guy do? He mows lawns." Without any touch of whining, he went on to tell how Chief Denton came to visit him. He said, "Yes right in my apartment and –"

Mrs. C. sat right forward in her chair and interrupted, "Chief Denton. Now there is a fine man. And handsome too, if I may say it. Sorry I didn't see him in the hall."

Willie replied, "Well I suppose he is. And he can sure make a point. He says something and you know that's it. So after the chief gave me the word, I went over to Rousseau's and told em I was done with it. Out of their lives and all. Can you believe it though, this Carol Girard, she pulled a gun right out on me." He passed on saying that he could see it was a small revolver like women might carry in a purse. Not a fine powerful Glock like his. He wondered if Mrs. C. knew that a revolver has a revolving cylinder and a pistol has a clip, or as Sarge at the range calls it, a magazine. He would have enjoyed asking her if she's seen any kid water pistols with a cylinder. Would a woman who drinks British style tea care about any of that? Not likely.

Mrs. C. drank the last of her tea, placed the cup on the table, wiped her fingers carefully with her napkin and said, "Well, guns are not always in a purse. I'm here alone and I suppose it is known around that I'm, shall we say, comfortable financially. I have my jewels and wear them to church or in town to lunch. I have a bank account in town naturally but sometimes –" She pushed her hand down between the cushions of her chair. Willie nearly fell out of his. "See," she said, "a nice little revolver just right for me. I have service people in for carpet cleaning, for tv, even a plumber last week. And I don't lock my door during the day. I mean we're really a nice small town and all. I watch tv you know. So just in case. My father was very comfortable with guns – and so am I." She carefully placed the .38 on her serving table and said, "Had this one long before Andre at Lavalle's opened his store to guns and ammunition. I hear he's doing a lively business. Glad to hear it. It is New Hampshire. We like our guns for the good things and sometimes we may need them for the bad ones."

Willie left Mrs. C with warmth from a pleasant cup of tea, three chocolate chip cookies enjoyed and near dizziness with his fantasy auntie – she who packs a gun! Amazing, he thought, same .38 that Carol G. showed. Small, lightweight. Women like em, it seems. The visit had made him feel good about himself. He got to tell his full story. She felt for him about that bullying when he was young. She had nodded several times in the Rousseau part. She understood that he was the aggrieved party, it seemed to him. He'd told her nothing about the new real plan though, just nice guy Willie who made his peace and was going on with his life.

15

It was a just a few days to Labor Day, the weekend that unofficially ended summer. For the town of Helios, it would be a weekend to remember. The grand official opening of the new Riverside Coos County Park and the celebration to mark the unique occasion. A traveling carnival was setting up featuring chance games and rides and a promise of great food stands. Cotton candy and popcorn required and a fireworks finale. Willie had stayed true to his word. No contact at all with the Rousseaus or that Carol and her gun. He would be patient and find his time. He didn't even know what his action would be. But he'd know it when the right time came. Maybe he'd even see them at the park celebration and give a big wave.

He worked his full day at the mulch site. Heavy boots carefully tied protecting around the huge logs that were ground to massive heaps of mulch. No camo attire. Owner and boss, Henry Storrow, was a Vietnam vet and Willie didn't need to be put on the spot about how he had served – especially since he hadn't. He had finished his supper, one of his favorite micros, the Salisbury Steak with mashed potatoes and a nice apple crisp for desert. Eaten right out of the container. Only a coffee cup to rinse out. His dishwasher was kept silent for days. The range oven was like new, and his utility bill stayed pleasantly low. Windows open, no AC for him.

Moving On

He watched the nightly tv news and began an old black and white western. Two beers, and he was starting to drift off in his recliner. Suddenly – loud pounding on his door. Bang! Bang! A rare thing for him! He instantly roused himself. He jumped up and rushed to the door. Eye hole sighting first. What! Mrs. C. out there! He opened and she half-stumbled through. She grasped the door frame and choked out, "Willie – I – I need help!"

He led her to a chair and said, "Mrs. C! Whatever is going on! Let me get you a glass of water. Just take your time. I am here to help."

She could only sit on the edge of the chair. Hand shaking, she took a few sips of water and struggled out her distress. "Just had to – to shoot the guy – ran off – think I got him in the leg – no, shoulder maybe – call 911 for me – intruder ran off – down our back fire exit stairs – some blood in the hall."

Willie always kept his cell phone at the ready. He pulled it out of his pocket and dialed 911.

Officer Ainsworth was there in minutes. Willie had the door open for him. The officer stopped and unholstered his weapon. He spoke directly to Willie, "You made the 911, right? You said a shooting. Is there a person with a weapon in there? A situation of danger?"

"No – no – this lady rushed down the hall from her apartment, pounded on my door pleading for help. Intruder burst in on her and – well – she shot him! She does not have the gun with her. She thinks she hit him, maybe leg or shoulder. Saw blood in the hall by the fire exit door. He got away through it."

Weapon held down in the ready position, Officer Ainsworth said, "You see to the victim. I am going to pursue out that exit. To see if he may have collapsed on the stairs or in his car. I'll be calling the chief at home. He will be right on this immediately also."

Willie went back to Mrs. C. "You heard the officer. You are in safe hands now for certain."

She had collapsed back into the chair nearly faint. She murmured, "Thank, you ... Thank you ... Willie."

In ten minutes Chief Denton was at the door and in full uniform. As he approached her chair, he said, "Intruder not on the premises so Officer Ainsworth is driving the area to spot a runner or car out of place."

~ ~ ~

Willie was starting to swell with importance – he was now a vital part of a crime scene. He rushed to the kitchen and brought in a chair. He said, "Here, Chief, maybe if you sit, she will feel more comfortable."

"Yes that can help. I see that she is naturally very distraught. He addressed her directly, "Oh, I know you. Mrs. Caniston, right? You own the building and live down the hall. I see you in town. Officer Ainsworth filled me in. But tell all you can. From the beginning."

Seeing the chief in full control, Mrs. C gained her poise and said, "Yes, I did shoot that man. At him anyway. Enough to make him turn and run. Meant to do more than that." She sipped her water again. Willie stood nearby and nodded vigorously to signal she was doing fine. She went on, "I have a legal pistol. You will know that. I forgot to lock my door as I usually do. Suddenly this masked guy whips it open. I was watching tv. and was completely shocked. I keep my gun right in the cushions in my chair. This proves it! Can never be too trusting these days."

"That's fine, so far. What did this intruder look like? What did he say?"

"It was all so sudden. But he was definitely not a tall person like you. Shorter, like Willie." She gestured to Willie who grimaced. She went on, "Had on what they call a hoodie, it was dark color, and he had a white handkerchief over his lower face. Stood right in front of me. No gun. Just this ugly knife. Long blade like for a hunter. He waved it as a terrifying threat. He said, 'Okay lady, I know you got jewels in this place. Probably cash too. On your feet and show me.' " I watch tv. I knew to distract. I swept my arm toward the bedroom. True to it – he turned to look." She paused to be sure it was right. "I quickly pulled my pistol from the cushions. He just stood there stunned for a few seconds. But still threatening. He moved closer. He snarled, 'Lady – don't be a fool. Drop that – or I'm gonna have to cut you up bad.' She sipped her water once more. "He had one of those pop out knife blades. Terrifying! So – I shot him. He howled and ran for the door. Would have got him full on but my hand is not what it used to be."

Chief got up from the chair and turned to Willie and said, "Willie Martin, it's good to see you on the right side of things now. You've done well here. Continue to see to her. I'm going to secure the scene at her apartment." He stooped to be sure she understood him and said, "I'm going to have to take your pistol in for evidence and testing, Mrs. Caniston. You will be without it for a while. The State Police will come in for blood DNA and their investigation." He reached and touched her arm. "We'll get this guy."

In better composure now, Mrs. C. said, "I'm not in any trouble am I? For shooting like that." She dabbed her forehead with a handkerchief. "I will never forget to lock my door again, that's for certain."

"No, no trouble assuming things are as you described them. A classic of self-defense it seems. Defending your castle, standing your ground. That's what those laws are for." He turned to go and at the door he said, "Did you acquire that gun at Lavalle's?"

"No, no not from Lavalle's. My husband bought that pistol some years back. Down state. I guess he knew something. He always said I might need it someday. That man was not right about too much, but he saved me today. Rest in Peace, Herbert."

~ ~ ~

Next day at the diner and at Lavalle's Hardware, the accounts of Mrs. Caniston's attempted robbery were all The Big News. A rare shooting crime for Helios. Most of the town's police calls were pathetic domestic violence and some drug arrests. The kids swiping out of the parent's cabinets at parties were rarely reported. Folks didn't want that risk public and even possible liability negligence. Northern states always had long-term investigations for smuggling of cigarettes out of Canada's close border. Beating the taxes. And public drunkenness by the usual suspects who got sober overnight in the station jail. At Lavalle's, townspeople gathered right at the gun counter and filled in with the exciting pieces they had heard. Accurate or not. And plenty of opinions: "This guy must live somewheres and that will show up. That Mrs. Caniston, I seen her down at the range. She's no one to challenge, looks like." – "See that! Guns are darn sure more than for hunting. Second Amendment is right again."

Back home after closing, Andre and Myra sat before

dinner with a glass of wine for her and a beer for him. Always a nice cold bottle, never a can. Settled on their back porch with cheese and crackers, Andre was in the Whew-what a day-mode. He took a full drink of his beer and said to his wife, "My Lord, Myra, I just can't sort it all out. I know Mrs. Caniston a bit, but I had no idea she would have a gun at her place. I hear it was a .38. She didn't buy it from us, I do know that."

"Well maybe this is one time I'd be glad if she did. Word is anyway, that guy is long gone. Probably into Canada by now. There's always a few passing through and hear stuff around. Diner's always good for some overhears. She sipped her wine and said, "Chief Denton and now the State Police, they won't give up on it."

Andre munched his cracker. "Crazy enough, this will be just great for our gun business. Total proof again that you need some home protection."

His wife nodded and added, "But I will say this, I hear that Mrs. Caniston had some proper training. I shudder to think about those who think just having a gun in the nightstand is all they need. Or the ones who leave loaded ones in closets with kids in the home. Next thing it will come with little Andy into the third grade one day." Myra stood and rubbed her arms. "It's cool already in the early evening. Yes, feels like a fall night with Labor Day coming this weekend. Let's finish inside."

Andre couldn't resist. He picked up his half empty beer raised it and said, Here's one for us – at the big park celebration, do you think they'll have one of those duck shooting games? They'd better for this timing."

16

At his apartment, Willie Martin dressed for the big park celebration event. He passed on the camo look for a simple blue work shirt and khakis. Boots laced this time. Maybe he'd need to run from "doing something." His jacket would seem right because the evenings were already getting cool. The jacket would of course be vital to cover his Glock. He'd had his concealed-carry permit now for over five years. It pleased him as an experienced gun owner to purchase rounds and a fine new holster at Lavalle's.

No more pushing the pistol into his waistband belt. He considered himself one tough guy. Could be that there'd be gun shots covered perfectly by the booms of tonight's fireworks. Great distraction if timed just right. The Commissioners had decided that there would be no alcohol sales at the event, but wasn't it likely that Rousseau would drift off from his happy little group, daughter and that Carol Girard. Maybe he'd slip back to his car at just the right time, for a needed slug of something stronger than carnival Pepsi. What would a guy like Rousseau drink for hard stuff, he wondered. Nice flask in the side pocket always worked.

Preparing for a night of pleasure, in his den Rodney looked up at the baseball trophies and anticipated again the special thrill of crowds and cheers. Tonight's celebration was no baseball game, but it would surely have crowds and excitement, and he'd be with the people he cared for. In the bedroom, Carol pulled on jeans and a tan sweatshirt for the cool evening. Then she carefully tucked the pistol into a belt pack. No purse in crowds, but the .38 had become her certain companion for out and around. In her room Tracy was bursting with pleasure – the end to a perfect summer and the start of her final school year. There had been no open talk of Dad and Carol moving on to marriage, but they certainly made a definite couple. They'd be three tonight giving her again a real sense of family.

If ever the Helios Diner had need for lively chatter, the attempted robbery and shooting and the park celebration were It for days. Mrs. Caniston's shooting was far more intriguing than the typical gossip or weather predictions. Sympathy for a respected local senior citizen ran deep. But a robber and her having a gun to shoot him – it was a sensation.

The chatter was lively especially since it was Labor Day. Locals filled the place for a late breakfast. They promised themselves to pass on lunch so they could indulge a night of pleasure foods at the park's opening celebration and carnival. By five o'clock half the town was gathered at the former Remy LeClair farm now known as the Riverside Coos County Park. Volunteer firefighters from the town directed traffic. Off the highway, a new paved parking lot stretched out along the parkland's edge. Cars were guided into neat rows, mostly 4-by-4 vehicles ready for the coming winter.

Adjacent to the parking lot a temporary platform had been structured. On it were two chairs, a podium and microphone. No chairs for the crowd. Commissioner Gradner would be brief. He knew he'd better be. Already kids were pulling on mom and dad's arms. Ready for its first riders, the Ferris wheel was brilliantly lighted and the smells of hot dogs and popcorn drifted to them. The Commissioner held up his hand to the big crowd for as much quiet as he could expect. He said, "Yes, kids, my talk will be short and – then we'll get on to the fun – rides, games, popcorn and cotton candy."

The Commissioner pointed to the rows of vehicles in the lot. "I want to thank the fire department volunteers for their expert handling of more traffic than Helios usually sees." He nodded to Chief Denton in the other chair, "Thank you Chief, for your faithful time being with us here tonight and always for your protection. You all should know that this park has a fine exercise trail now with stops for special workouts. You can jog or walk all the way down to the river, sit on a bench, catch your breath. drink from the water bottle you'd be sure to carry and contemplate the scene. In winter, the park will be open for cross-country skiing, snowshoeing and snowmobiles. We are here tonight to celebrate the great New Hampshire Life. Let's go do it!"

Lights sparkled on all the rides, games and food stands. From speakers, classic carnival music filled the air. Kids ran about pointing to their favorites. Lines formed quickly at the popcorn stand and for the absolutely required cotton candy. Carefree Carnival Company was rented for the event traveling up from Nashua. They had been in Vermont for three days and were willing to do a single good-cause night in their touring schedule. By state fair levels, it was a small setup with a share of the fees returned to the county for park maintenance. No farm animals or crop exhibits but there was the fine Ferris wheel. On the carousel for the kids, choose to ride a shiny white horse, a happy brown dog, a billy goat or even a plump, pink pig. Before the ride they will absolutely need an airbrush tattoo to show off.

The local and famous I-Scream had a booth for soft serve, soft drinks and had added candied apples. Hot dogs and hamburgers were offered right from the grill by – of course the Helios Diner. There were games from ring toss and dart balloons, baseball throws and yes, a duck shooting range. They all featured a dazzling row of stuffed animals for prizes from small green bullfrogs, to brown monkeys with white faces and curled tails and the inevitable giant teddy bears. "You betcha – prize every time!" was the vendor's invitation to everyone who passed by.

Logan and Kristen were back from college for the holiday weekend. He was in his Dartmouth green sweatshirt and she in the Middlebury blue and white with her ponytail popping out of the back of her cap. With Kurt and Jocelyn they strolled about stopping to wave to friends and soaking in the delights of it all. When they came to it, Logan would not let them pass up the hot dog-hamburger stand. As they moved to the line, Kristen made sure that Jocelyn heard her comment, "Well, what a surprise, Logan has not lost his appetite to books and term papers. He does love an excuse to eat."

Kurt offered his take, "Hey, I heard that too. He's no little brother any more, is he? What? At now six-two, one ninety? Shoulda tried out for the football team. They always need all the help they can get in that tough Ivy League."

"Never would have made it, but Dartmouth has a great

running track in the stadium. I run it four times a week. I keep my head busy with classes and my body fed and exercised." He reached for Kristen's arm and gave a gentle squeeze. He said, "Lots of my free time is taken up with emails and calls to a certain friend of mine. If I have a car on campus next year, it could even find its way to Middlebury College on some weekends."

Kristen nodded and smiled her best "I accept" smile.

Tracy spotted Amy and it seemed the timing was perfect – her best friend to be with and a chance for Dad and Carol to hold hands and be a couple. Tracy and Amy headed for the Ferris wheel and after the line moved up, they were guided by the controller safely to their open pods. They settled into the seats and were glad they had waited for the candied apples. Maybe not good to be eating up there. Every pod was lively with kids and moms and dads. As the giant wheel slowly moved to the top, Amy said, "See that, your Air Force career has already begun. Whoa! We're at the highest point now, the apex, that great term from geometry classes."

"And look at that view! The fall foliage is ready to show itself. This line along the exercise trail will be bursting with red and yellow soon." Tracy pointed to the south of the property. "See that's the red barn on the farm where I spent my summer with the Slaters. You can see all the way to the river. We could easily walk down to it and have a picnic along the banks under the elms. Me and Jocelyn did it twice. We had great times together and she taught me a lot, like, you know, about life."

Amy scanned the grounds and waved to anyone who looked up. She said, "You aren't afraid of heights are you?"

She laughed and punched Tracy's shoulder in fun. "It's an Air Force joke. But look at those kids in the one ahead. Dad is having a tough time keeping them from craning heads over the side."

Tracy pointed to the thick bank of clouds along the Vermont horizon. Crows were perched in the branches of the huge elms that lined the property. The birds flapped, cawed out as if resentful of all the goings on in peaceful Remy farmland. She turned to Amy and held her arm tightly and said, "At this time next week we will have been three days in classes. Senior year! We've been like such great friends since elementary. Let's always keep connected no matter our – our who-knows-what."

"This Ferris wheel ride will be our launching pad." After two trips around, Tracy said, "Actually I am getting a bit woozy from this motion. Maybe we need food!" At the bottom turn, they slipped off the ride and were helped to the exit platform. The girls stood back away from the Ferris wheel and watched the blinking lights and took their fun now waving to the riders.

Rodney and Carol wandered over to the duck shooting gallery and looked on while Ed Castuss pinged the metal ducks off as they spun by. Ed was famous for his hunting skills and had some impressive buck antlers trophies mounted on the walls of his den. He put down the game rifle and laughed, "See that – no real challenge – too easy for me." He turned to Carol and said, "Go ahead, you pick the prize. My kids are all too old now." Carol chose a chubby panda bear thinking that Tracy would crowd it in with her other stuffed ones on her bed, specials gathered over her young years.

Ed made a grand sweeping gesture to hand the rifle to Rodney. "Here ya go, let's see what ya got. Maybe another prize for the lady." Never the shy one or willing to be always "the lady," Carol gently took the rifle from Rodney and said, "Actually, I'm the shooter in this couple."

"She's right, you know." Rodney did not make any macho defense to salvage his pride. He passed the gun over to Carol and said, "No hunter's skill for me. But when we get to the baseballs and milk bottles – watch out!"

Carol set the game's rifle in the proper light grip and took her stance. The bright yellow ducks swam and quacked along the painted track waves. They moved at a rapid rate requiring serious skill to hit them. Carol banged down one after another as they sped by. Ed gaped, his face popping with amazement. "Man," he said, "this lady is crack a shot. I need her with a shotgun at night to guard my chicken coops up at the farm. That blasted fox would have no chance. Yes indeedy, 'blasted' is the right word."

With panda bear twins under her arm, Carol and Rodney headed for the food stands. "Hot dog right off the grill with mustard and sauerkraut and a nice Coke. Sounds about right." Rodney pretended to be a kid tugging at his mother.

Carol pulled him to a stop and said, "That does sound perfect. Especially since we skipped lunch. Maybe some chips too." She held her arms close to her body and said, "Why don't you get us a table spot while I go back to the car to leave these panda prizes and for my jacket. That fall chill is already here for me. Besides I have great leather to show off."

Days before the celebration it constantly buzzed in

Moving On

Willie Martin's mind at night as he sat with his beer. After all those cruelties and rejections from school with no way to get even, he somehow needed this one to be happen. He had no real plan, but he was sure he'd know it when it came. Mrs. C. loved the word "fortuitous" and urged him to use it when it was right. Tonight he had promised himself that there'd be something fortuitous for certain. He had seen Rodney and Carol strolling about enjoying the celebration. And why not, that new and gentler Willie Martin had stayed off just as he said he would.

Willie made certain that they did not spot him as he mixed with the crowds. It had excited him to be a stalker so exquisitely innocent. A stalker – just like in the movies. He watched the marked couple approach the food stand. His alert signals totally buzzed when Carol eased away. Yes! She was headed back to the parking area. He kept his distance carefully and watched as she followed along the car lines. Of course, they had driven in her Impala, space for his daughter to come along.

It was just too easy. Willie observed the interior lights in the car coming up. He was close enough now to see her reach into the back and slide a jacket over the front seat. Then she closed the car door and clicked the alarm signal. The interior lights dimmed out. He watched as she stopped to run the zipper up on her jacket. As she moved away from the car – now or never – he leaped out and blocked her way. He snarled, "Well now – one time – some perfect luck for me! Guess you know me by now – Ms. Carol herself and in her fine leather jacket." He looked her up and down and laughed. "Leather, huh? It sure looks great on you."

Stunned in the spot, Carol was speechless. Willie held

his ground with hands on hips – finally a man totally in charge. Carol tried to ease to the left as if passing a stranger. He moved in stride to block. Like kids on a playground. Carol feigned confidence straining to knock down any signal of fear. She looked directly at him. She said, "Willie Martin – you know this already looks like assault. There's no going back now."

"Ah you're wrong there. Nobody around. Ain't gonna hurt you. Just your word 'gainst mine."

"What ever happened to that 'I'm out of your lives' thing back on Rodney's lawn?"

Willie moved in closer, threatening but careful not to touch. He savored the moment. "So you bought that, right? Don't believe all what ya hear. Let's take it back to that very first time for us. Back there at the baseball park. Old Rodney just hadda play hero." Willie touched his cap and pulled himself up taller. He leaned in closer nearly to her face and smirked, "Maybe you just chose the wrong guy. Me 'n you could of been – well guess we'll never know, will we?"

Then instantly Willie saw the move. Gripped and whisked out of the holster – he pointed his Glock right at her. He stepped back to give space. "So – I'm guessing you got that slick little revolver right in your pack there tonight. Last time I saw that weapon – you was standing right on Rodney's steps with his kid there too. Take your hand away – very careful now."

The voice was firm. The order was absolutely clear. "Right behind you, Willie Martin. Reach down now – real easy. Place that weapon right on the ground." Chief Denton stepped around in front of Willie. His Glock was steady on. He said, "You think I haven't been watching you all night?

With all your history with these people. Must have seen me. Now up against that car door. Hands behind your back. Somehow, I think you know the drill."

The chief so tall – and him so small. Willie knew it was over. He heard his rights, those famous words so common on his tv shows. He was now officially and totally arrested – for this foolish show of – what was it now – hurt pride and a need to get even for a pathetic grudge. He had let the humiliation fester in his mind until he could not even tell what was reality and what was desperation to show courage, a courage crushed to the ground all those years. And now permanently.

After he and Officer Ainsworth led Willie to the police cruiser, the chief came back to Carol who was nearly collapsed on to the hood of her car. He made certain she was not hurt. He needed to be sure she was trying to ease down from this terrifying threat. Now standing and regaining her sense of it all, she said, "So weird, isn't it. Actually, I feel sorry for the guy. I wanted to believe he really was going to leave us alone. Just like he said last time we saw him." As soon as that gun came out, I knew he was well beyond any real hope." She looked directly at the chief and said, "It's not going to be good for him, is it?"

"No, it is definitely not going to be good. You are right – an open gun threat is a whole different category. And for certain, no self-defense claim here. When he gave that good support to Mrs. Caniston, maybe that will help some." He put his arm around her shoulder and said, "Go back and be with Rodney and enjoy the rest of the celebration as much as you can. Let him comfort you. And don't miss the great fireworks they have planned. Come in tomorrow and we will work on your statement. Willie Martin is not going anywhere."

~ ~ ~

"Let him comfort you" was still in Carol's mind. No surprise from his style, but Carol deeply appreciated the direct rescue from crazy Willie and the Chief's lingering kindness. Yes, she pulled in to Rodney's arm that was clamped tightly around her shoulder. Kristen, Kurt and Logan slid in together with them for the excitement to watch the grand finale fireworks. Tracy and Amy came waving and running from one last Ferris wheel ride. As they ran, they tried to balance paper cups from sloshing the final precious gulps of soda.

~ ~ ~

The best viewing spots were in the parking lot away from the carnival lights and Ferris wheel. Excited kids pulled on parents to find the perfect one. Some, most likely adults, went to their cars to honk approval of the bursts. It was called "vehicle applause." No kid would be content with that lumpy sequestered location. Open clapping and jumping with buddies was required. How would you face classmates without the fireworks displays in your carnival stories.

~ ~ ~

Volunteers from the fire department clearly practiced the rigid safety procedures needed. They set off the first rockets with long igniters. Rocket trails zoomed across the black star-sprinkled sky. Kids screamed delight and car horns honked approval. Living for years the other adjacent side to the Remy farm property time, two ladies with great kindness and love for animals had for some months adopted shelter dogs. Some were from nearby towns and some even brought in from southern states. Found on the internet. There were up to over a dozen dogs now, and their place had become a favorite drive visit. Just like pet farms you could go inside the fence with Janice and Ellen there out for approval. Of course the dogs of all sizes and types would rush up knowing that treats from pockets were certain. Dogs hate loud noises and doubled with repeated booms sent them howling and into the overhead shelters the women had crafted. Thunderstorms always brought the same fearful retreats as well.

~ ~ ~

In the parking lot some of the children had the same fears of the boom levels. In strollers they cried and instinctively clamped their hands over their ears. Moms and dads leaned in to comfort and a few had to retreat to their cars. Amy turned to Tracy and pointed at one stroller, "Oh that's little Andrew Milton. I baby sit for him sometimes. I'm going over to help if I can." Mom was already bending in to Andrew. When she looked up and saw Amy, she said, "Look Andy, it's your favorite friend Amy. Yes she was with you at your swings just yesterday." Andy stopped crying and stretched his arms out toward Amy. Back with Tracy, Amy was downright pleased with herself for a quick save and that Andy clearly cared for her. Tracy nudged her friend's shoulder, "See that, a little kid showing up his mother already."

~ ~ ~

The displays were set for twenty minutes. The grand finale was the classic fountains, a rainbow of sparks floating down from giant cone shapes in the sky.

First a hush in the crowd at the spectacular bursts. Then shouting, clapping and car honking followed for several minutes. Commissioner Gradner rushed forward to the crowd. He motioned for the volunteers to come out for a bow. He made no attempt to be heard but everyone applauded. No one hurt and a perfect ending to the night's celebration. It would likely be in Helios lore for years to come.

17

It was almost more amazing news than any small town could handle. But they cherished every moment trying. At a quiet breakfast at home, Carol insisted on pancakes with fresh New Hampshire blueberries. Batter by Tracy and flipped in the pan with expert baseball skills by Rodney. At one point Rodney fastened on Carol's eyes directly. He asked, "Well, now you need to tell us all of it – with strange Willie Martin last night, what did you think was actually going to happen – what if you'd really been able to get your .38 out? My God – what – a deadly shootout?" Tracy turned from drying dishes and leaned in for the answer.

~ ~ ~

Carol remained silent for a long time. She slid her finger around the edge of her coffee cup. Twice. Yet again. Finally she answered, "You said it, Rodney – my God."

~ ~ ~

Up at the Slater farm, Kurt and Roselyn, Logan and Kristen tried to sort the night out at their own breakfast. Logan had invited Kristen to be with them. They were both returning to college the next morning. All so nearly bizarre – dangerous Willie Martin with direct ties to Tracy, Jocelyn's eager summer helper. Yet the night was amazingly balanced by delight of the celebration. There was far more meaning for them than the great fireworks finale. For these four, it was the passing of the Remy LeClair farm. From last night on, it had become a place of pleasure for all the town of Helios to enjoy.

~ ~ ~

After the scrambled eggs and bacon, the rye toast and the coffee, Kurt said, "Bring your coffee. Let's go into the studio and salute Harry and Lillian." In the studio, they stood facing the *Apple Blossoms* painting by now famous grandson James Kaiser. It had been hung back in its original place. They looked yet again at that beautiful little girl holding the gentle white blossoms to her face. Kurt raised his cup. He said, "Here's to the great tradition of the farm owned by Harry and Lillian Kaiser and cared for by us with such," he searched for the words, and found one not easy for him, 'such love.' And to their care for the people who have passed through this property. They shared its gifts." There were smiles and nods all around.

The End

Acknowledgements

Thank you New Hampshire for my peaceful and healthy roots. I was able to provide details in this novel for the famous Aerial Tramway and the Old Man in the Mountain because as a college summer job, I worked as a summer tourist guide on the mountain trails. Then on to Plymouth Teachers College (now PSU) for more of the world view in that glorious local setting. Also, growing up in the small NH town of Littleton, I was certainly aware of guns. No locals were packin' and being aroused to shootouts. But Deer Season opening was a like a holiday and some kids skipped school for it. The deer kill provided trophies for car roof tops and for serious meat throughout the year – and for ecological control of ticks and endless assault on farmers' gardens.

The section covering the fictional house fire and rescue was totally written by my grandson Adam Birkmier who had extensive fire and rescue training. Also, Adam had been composing stories since third grade, for class – and with Grandpa's encouragement

About the Author

Larry Presby grew up in the White Mountains of New Hampshire, taught English at Southold High School and Sayville High School, both on Long Island. He graduated from Plymouth State University and University of Massachusetts; served in the New Hampshire and New York National Guard. He acted in the Lincoln, New Hampshire Summer Theatre. He and his wife Rosemarie divide their time between Baldwinsville, New York, and Spring Hill, Florida. Larry enjoys writing, photography, golf and hearing from his former students. He has three children and five grandchildren.

The New Atlantian Library

NewAtlantianLibrary.com
or AbsolutelyAmazingeBooks.com
or AA-eBooks.com